Loving the BILLIONAIRE ARMY DOC

dobi daniels

Luxhaven
Publishing

To JC, Grandma D, and DG, whom I love more than life itself.

Thank you for choosing LOVING THE BILLIONAIRE ARMY DOC. I enjoyed writing the story of Jasmine Banks and David Landi, inspired by a topic dear to my heart.

It's so easy to believe your life is over when you are faced with dire circumstances, becoming convinced that love cannot come your way again. I pray LOVING THE BILLIONAIRE ARMY DOC gives you the hope to believe that love is still possible no matter what life hands you.

Please continue this journey with me in LOVING THE BILLIONAIRE BOSS DOC, which is the story about Gabriella Landi, David's sister. You can grab your copy at https://dobidaniels.com.

Would you like to be notified when the next Dobi Daniels book releases? Sign up at https://dobidaniels.com.

Once again, thank you so much for purchasing LOVING THE BILLIONAIRE ARMY DOC and for meeting Jasmine Banks and David Landi. If you enjoyed it, please consider leaving a review at your favorite retailer or recommending it to a friend.

Thanks again for your support!

Dobi Daniels

Loving the BILLIONAIRE ARMY DOC

CHAPTER 1

Jasmine Banks' heart ached with the knowledge of her recent discovery as she rolled her carry-on luggage behind her and exited the arrival gate at Dexington International Airport. The area teemed with people of all ages and all races moving in different directions. But she felt alone, trapped in her new reality.

She'd taken a week's vacation after she finished her latest ObGyn rotation to attend the New York Bridal Fashion Week at her mother's insistence. Jasmine's parents, Edward and Leah Banks, owned IntimiRose, a high-end boutique lingerie company that produced some of the most highly sought-after lingerie designs on the east coast. IntimiRose had been in her mother's family for many generations and was known for its innovative and stylish yet comfortable whimsical floral designs. Jasmine's mom usually attended the fashion shows but had pleaded with Jasmine to go on her behalf this time around.

It had, for the most part, been a wonderful trip. Jasmine couldn't remember when last she'd been in New York for a fashion show, and it had been fun to see the latest trends in bridal wear. She'd taken copious notes and snapped pictures which were sure to make her mother happy. Even the brunette wig and brown contacts she'd worn to fulfill a dare she had with her roommate, Dana Adams, hadn't bothered her. Thank goodness that dare would be over in a week's time, and then she'd be back to her comfy redhead and beautiful green eyes.

She'd even met Gabriella Landi, a high school friend she'd lost touch with over the years, and they had caught up, though they'd avoided talking about the elephant in the room that was her brother, Tony Landi. Jasmine and Tony had dated in high school before the relationship had imploded and he'd left town for college. But it had been good to see Gabriella again. They'd agreed to reconnect back in Dexington where she still lived. Jasmine had thought the week one of the best times in her life.

But what she had discovered last night had soured the trip and driven sleep from her eyes. In the past few months, Jasmine had watched her roommates and best friends, Alicia Montgomery and Dana Adams, fall in love and get their happily-ever-afters. For a moment, she'd hoped it meant she had a chance for one too—despite her desire to keep her heart locked up—because blessings came in triples, right? But that dream had been crushed by the lump she'd discovered in her right breast while taking a shower last night.

For some women, it would have been nothing more than a benign lump given her young age of twenty-eight. But it was a possible death knell for Jasmine. She had found out at her maternal grandmother's death bed a few years ago that they had some East European Jewish heritage. Which wouldn't have meant anything, except that Jasmine had already read about how the BRCA gene mutation, a precursor for hereditary breast and ovarian cancers, was common among this specific Jewish ancestry.

Given that her grandmother's sister had died from breast cancer, Jasmine had convinced her family to undergo genetic testing. The results had shown that Jasmine and her mom had inherited the BRCA2 gene mutation, though her aunt—her mom's only sister and sibling—hadn't. But since her mom had been screened regularly since then and no cancer cells had been found so far, Jasmine had assumed the same might happen for her and had even entertained the hope for love after seeing Alicia and Dana blossom in it.

Since the testing, Jasmine had done everything humanly possible to minimize her risk, short of changing her genetic makeup. She'd had bi-yearly checkups, had been religious about what she ate or drank, had avoided any bad habits, and had always kept her body in top shape. And even though there had been no evidence that any of these helped to reduce her risk of cancer, she'd hoped her regimen and lifestyle might make a difference. But all that might have been in vain.

Of course, the next logical step was to inform

her gynecologist and book an appointment at the breast clinic—she of all people should know what to do given her medical training. A classic 'physician, heal thyself' scenario, right? But that didn't stop Jasmine from being afraid of what the results might reveal, the reality of what she might have to face, and the possibility that she might never achieve any of her dreams.

She'd been looking forward to finishing her obstetrics and gynecology residency which should happen in a little over a year's time. She also had plans to begin a fellowship in Gynecologic Oncology once the residency ended, if she was accepted for the spot. It had been a big dream of hers—helping women who might be afflicted with hereditary breast or ovarian cancer. Now, there was a good chance she might not even make it to the end of the year, depending on the results of the lump biopsy. And there was no guarantee the lump wouldn't reoccur.

She adjusted the sunglasses over her face so no one would see her swollen eyes. She'd cried on and off last night and had done her best to hide the evidence this morning, but she wasn't sure how good of a job her makeup was doing.

So the sunglasses were staying on till she got home.

Jasmine sighed. This was now her new reality, one she couldn't run away from. Thinking about it would not get rid of the lump. It sat there as a constant reminder of the horrible future that awaited her. She needed hope, anything, a glimpse of an alternate future. *God, I need You.*

Something bumped into her and Jasmine found herself landing on her butt on the floor. Pain shot through her ankle as her feet hit something solid. *Ouch!*

"I'm so sorry. Are you okay?" Jasmine looked up to see startling brown eyes with gold flecks in them staring at her with concern. The man that extended a hand to her cut a handsome figure with his chiseled features and well-toned build encased in a black T-shirt, blue jeans, and a grey military style jacket. He sported a modified crew cut with longer hair at the top, which paired with the aviator glasses he wore, gave him a dashing look that Jasmine found alluring.

She accepted his hand and he pulled her to her feet. Jasmine felt a jolt in her heart as sparks of electricity shot through her arm as their hands touched. *What just happened?* It had been a long time since any man had this kind of effect on her. And he looked familiar, like someone she'd known a long time ago, though she couldn't recollect who. But that wasn't possible—she would have remembered someone this attractive.

"Thank you," she said as she tested her ankle to make sure it was alright. It seemed to be okay. "I didn't see you there for a moment. Sorry about that."

He chuckled. "No worries. I wasn't looking either." A dimple appeared on his left cheek as he smiled at her. His citrusy sandalwood scent wove such a number around her that she felt the urge to stay and breathe it in.

Jasmine's heart rate picked up its pace. She never liked to use the word, but this guy fit the term "hot" to a tee. Her eyes darted to his fingers. No ring or ring marks, so possibly single. Now, here was a great catch for any girl, if his character was anything to match.

Hold on. Was he the answer to her quick prayer? Jasmine shook her head. No way. That was impossible. This was just her mind running ahead of itself. And she knew nothing about him. He could be a rapist for all she knew, though something told her that was not the case.

Besides, she had no business being interested in a guy with the horrible prognosis that faced her. Time to forget him, like she'd done for all the other guys that had approached her over the years. Jasmine had been too afraid of the possibility of cancer to allow any guy get close to her. And she'd been right to do so, considering what she'd just found out.

Her phone rang. Just in the nick of time. "Excuse me," she said as she pulled her phone from her jacket pocket. She pressed the answer button. "Hello, Mom."

"Where are you?" her mom asked from the other end of the line.

"We just deplaned. Could you hold on for one second?" Jasmine turned back to the guy who by now had righted her luggage, which had collapsed in a heap with his. "Thank you for your help," she said to him. She grabbed her luggage. "Have a good day."

"Same to you," he responded. "It was my pleasure."

She gave him a small wave and headed towards the security exit. "I'm back, Mom."

"What was that all about?"

"Nothing. I just collided into someone on my way out. But everything is fine."

"Okay, thank goodness. I'm outside by the pickup area."

Jasmine halted her steps. Her mother had never come to pick her up from the airport. "You didn't have to come. You should have sent Jerry." Jerry was her parents' chauffeur.

"I had something I wanted to discuss with you on the way home."

Jasmine started walking again. Interesting. What was it that her mom wanted to talk about that couldn't wait till she got home? Jasmine took the escalator that led to the baggage claim area. This wasn't good. Her mom was a total ninja at knowing when something was wrong. And that was the last thing Jasmine needed.

She couldn't let her find out about the lump. It would devastate her family and poison any last good memories she could make with them if the cancer had already advanced to a late stage. And Jasmine deserved those memories. So she had to be careful. "Okay, I'll be right there in a few minutes." She ended the call.

But first, a quick detour to the ladies was in order. Jasmine had to make sure her makeup was still in place, hiding the glaring proof of last night's meltdown.

Then it was time to see if her concealer application skills were as good as she believed.

avid Landi had been preoccupied with his thoughts when he'd bumped into the beautiful young lady wearing a cream-colored turtleneck tucked into form-fitting jeans and paired with high heeled ankle boots. Yes, she was stunning with a chic bob that only served to highlight her glowing skin, pert nose, and long eyelashes. Only someone without eyes would think otherwise. She looked up at him through dark sunglasses that only added to her loveliness.

"I'm so sorry. Are you okay?" he asked as he reached out a hand to help her up.

She took his hand, hers small yet fitting just right in his that he felt a hesitation to let it go.

But she might think him a pervert if he didn't. So he released her hand.

"Thank you," she said. "I didn't see you there for a moment. Sorry about that." Then her phone rang. "Excuse me." She turned to answer her call.

Their green-brown Globe-Trotter hand luggages had crashed into each other, so he pulled hers up before righting his. Interesting that they had similar tastes.

He watched her tuck an errant piece of hair behind her ear. Just like someone he'd known long ago in another life. But lots of people had this same mannerism.

She soon finished her call, thanked him, and headed toward the security exit. He felt a loss as he watched her walk away and disappear down the escalator, like he'd wanted her to stay and chat more with him.

David picked up his luggage. This was nuts. She was a total stranger and had nothing to do with him. Was he so starved for female attention because he'd been in the Army for so long? No, that couldn't be the case. He'd done just fine there.

He shook his head and started for the security exit. This was not the time and place to be thinking about another woman, or anything else for that matter. David took a deep breath and looked around the busy airport as he headed down the escalator. He was finally back in Dexington.

The last time he'd been here had been the Christmas before Heather, the love of his life, died. He'd finished his plastic surgery residency and had flown home to the east coast to celebrate with his family and introduce Heather to his parents. It had been the best Christmas of his life. And then they had both returned to Los Angeles to plan for their wedding.

But it had ended up their last holiday together. The pain from missing her still hurt like it had happened yesterday. Heather had been diagnosed with pancreatic cancer a few months after they'd returned, and he'd watched helplessly as she passed away three weeks later.

A part of him had died in the moment when her coffin was lowered into the grave. He'd poured himself into his reconstructive micro-surgery fellowship at UCLA to numb the pain, but the intense training hadn't been enough. He'd almost gone crazy from being around everything that reminded him of her, so he'd signed up for the Army and shipped off to Germany as soon as he completed his fellowship.

But it had been a good decision despite the circumstances. His skills had saved many wounded soldiers, and it had been the healing he'd needed. He'd felt a piece of himself come back alive with each patient he saved from the brink of death. And once his three-year stint with the Army was up, he'd considered going home. A call from his mother had sealed the deal. His father had suffered a stroke, so could he return?

And so here he was, back to pursue his dreams again—doing reconstructive micro-surgery and supporting the family business, though he'd felt overwhelmed at the thought of returning to Dexington and living a normal life again. He'd been able to secure an Assistant Professorship position at Dexington Medical Center and was expected to start work on Monday. And he still had an advisory role at Landisil Silicone, the billion-dollar company he'd founded with the silicone research that had been his brainchild in college—David held the patents to a silicone variant and its manufacturing process that reduced the leaching effect common with most silicone on the market.

Landisil Silicone now supplied silicone and its products to markets all over the world. It had entered the lingerie underwire business in recent years, where it now held a sixty percent share of the US market. Even though his sister supported his dad in running the company and they had a great management team, David knew it was not enough—his presence was still needed.

And that was all he wanted to focus on. Relationships didn't fit into his schedule, and he didn't need one to feel whole again. He still missed Heather with a deep ache, though it didn't hurt as much as before. Sometimes, David couldn't believe she was gone. Heather was probably the only woman he would ever love.

So, there was no room for anyone else in his life, even though a small part of him wanted to see the brunette lady again.

David looked at his watch and lengthened his strides. He would be late for breakfast if he didn't hurry. He'd taken the red-eye flight from Germany just to make sure he arrived on time. His mom had insisted on the breakfast, and when he'd called his parents as soon as he'd landed, they had hinted they had something important to discuss with him.

But he had no idea what that could be.

Time to find out.

CHAPTER 3

Jasmine stashed her luggage into the trunk of her mother's black Lexus SUV and slid into the front passenger seat after removing her sunglasses. Her mom, Leah Banks, ended the call she had been on and gave her a hug.

Dressed in a long black cardigan over a pink dress shirt, her mom looked younger than her late fifties with her glowing skin and unlined face. Very chic, just like the car interior with its custom pink and grey leather seats. People sometimes thought they were sisters rather than mother and daughter with their matching warm beige skin, the only difference being that her mother had long dark hair and brown eyes.

Jasmine had inherited her red hair and green eyes from her maternal grandmother.

"Hi, Mom!" Jasmine said. She gave her mom an air kiss on both cheeks. Her mom's familiar coconut rose scent swirled around her.

"How was New York?" her mom asked as she moved the car from the curb and joined the traffic leading away from the airport. She made no comments about Jasmine's eyes. Good. The makeup retouch must have worked its magic.

"It was great. Lots of new designs. I'll send you the pictures and my notes later," Jasmine responded in a voice that was chirpier than normal. Anything to prevent her mom from guessing how she truly felt. She leaned back into her seat. "How were your meetings, the ones you couldn't get away from?"

Her mom shot her a glance. "That's what I wanted to talk to you about."

What did that mean? Jasmine was not involved in the day-to-day running of Intimi-Rose even though she'd grown up around the business. How could her mom's meetings have anything to do with her?

"Landisil Silicone reached out to us about acquiring our business," her mom said.

Jasmine threw her mom a sharp look. "I didn't know you and dad were looking to sell." IntimiRose had been around forever as far as Jasmine was concerned. She couldn't imagine life in her family without it.

Her mom stared straight ahead. "We are not. They approached us to see if we were interested in a joint venture. Landisil entered the under-wire business a couple of years ago with their silicone product, and it ended up being a very successful move for them. Now they want to give back by targeting women who have had breast reconstruction and have a hard time finding the right lingerie. As you know, their skin becomes more sensitive post-surgery, making most bras hard to wear.

"One hundred percent of the profits from the joint venture would be used to support breast cancer research. We were excited when they shared what they had in mind, and the numbers made business sense. Then we talked a little further and discovered that they would have preferred to acquire our business outright but still run it as a separate brand. We wouldn't have considered it normally, but you know we have no one to inherit the business. You have chosen to be a gynecologist, and your aunt is not interested."

True. Her aunt, Rebecca Scott, had shown no interest in the fashion company. She'd mentioned getting involved would stifle her creativity and life. Jasmine's aunt was a socialite and a brilliant event planner whenever the urge hit her. She'd inherited enough money to keep her set for life and had managed to double that with her event planning. She didn't need to work five days a week if she didn't want to.

"But this business has been in our family for generations, so it's hard for us to let it go," her mom continued. "Then the owners of Landisil Silicone came up with an option we figured would work for everyone. And that's where you come in."

Jasmine knew how much her family cherished the business. Still, that didn't concern her. "Me? What are you talking about?"

"We would like you to marry their son. That way, your kids can still inherit IntimiRose."

Jasmine felt like cold water had been poured over her and she flinched. "Are you kidding? Mom, That's not funny!"

Her mom glanced at her before returning her

eyes on the road. "Hear me out first. It's not really an arranged marriage like you think. You'll have three weeks to go on arranged dates with him after which you'll decide if you want to go ahead with the marriage. If it doesn't work out after three weeks, then you can walk away. But you have to give it a real chance."

"But, Mom—"

"I know, I know." Her mom patted her hand. "I'm aware this is the twenty-first century. But the only reason your dad and I decided to consider it was when we discovered you were already familiar with their son. He is not a total stranger to you."

"And who might this gem be?" Jasmine asked in a sarcastic tone.

"Tony Landi."

Jasmine's heart dropped and she gripped the door handle. She didn't know whether to laugh or cry. It couldn't be. Definitely not Tony Landi. Yes, they'd known each other, but hadn't her mom also heard the part about how things had ended terribly between them? The memories of that time in her life were ones she had no plans to relive. He was now a total stranger as far as she was concerned. "Mom, no way!"

"I heard you liked him."

Jasmine turned to her mom. "Liked him? Mom, did you drink anything strange today? I want nothing to do with him! You couldn't pay me a million dollars to marry him."

"How about two million?"

"Mom!"

"Jasmine, just give it a chance. You know how they say hate is love in disguise. And I heard there might have been a misunderstanding."

"Not in this case. And I'm not getting married. This, whatever you guys call it, is not happening."

Her mom glanced at her before turning her eyes back on the road. By now, they were approaching the tollgate and then would enter the highway that led to the city. "If I remember correctly, a certain somebody promised Grandma on her deathbed that she'd take care of her business."

Jasmine had always had a feeling that promise would come back to bite her one day. "Mom, this is so unfair! I was only a teenager then."

"Promises are promises, young lady, especially a dying wish," her mom replied. "You should never make promises you don't mean or plan to keep. And who knows? You might fall for him. And it's only for three weeks. Any longer and the news about the possible deal could leak out. Jasmine, please give it a chance. You owe your grandmother that."

Jasmine rubbed her forehead. She could feel a headache coming on. "Could we forget this? My life is already stressful enough as it is. I don't need anything else to complicate it."

Her mom glanced at her. "Are you alright, dear?" Her eyes searched Jasmine's face with concern. "You look pale."

Jasmine looked away. "I'm fine," she said. She couldn't allow her mom to find out what was wrong. She could feel her mom's ninja instinct rearing its head. There was only one way to stop her digging any further.

She let out an exhale. "Okay, I'll do it. I'll go on the arranged date or whatever you're calling it," she said.

Her mom's face split into a grin. "Awesome! We've already set up dinner for you both on Friday evening. I'll send you the details later."

"So, my opinion wasn't going to change

anything, right? Seeing how you guys have everything all planned out."

"Your opinion absolutely matters, dear, but I knew I could convince you to go. I was ready to bribe you with that Hermès Birkin bag I just received if needed."

Jasmine perked up. "No way. I can still have it, can't I?"

"No, dear. Doctors don't need such expensive handbags."

"We still have lives outside the hospital you know."

Her mom nodded. "Yes, but not with my handbag."

Jasmine chuckled. Her mom could be funny sometimes.

"Thanks for agreeing to do this, dear," her mom said. "It means a lot to your dad and me."

Jasmine turned away to look out the window. This was not the way she had envisioned her morning would go. If anyone had told her this would happen, she would have laughed them off. What was she thinking going on an arranged-marriage date with Tony Landi, the one guy she despised, especially at this time when she had a life-and death-situation staring her in the face? *God, is this some sort of joke? What's going on here?* It was like her life was suddenly raining hailstones.

She leaned back into the headrest and closed her eyes. Well, maybe one good thing would come out of it—the chance to finally find out the truth about what had happened so many years ago. To lay that ghost to rest so to speak. But was it worth the anguish of seeing Tony Landi again?

Jasmine blew out a long sigh.

What had she gotten herself into?

CHAPTER 4

*D*avid entered his parents' living room and dropped his hand luggage on the marble floor before walking over to where his mom stood waiting. He leaned forward and gave her a kiss on the cheek. "Hi, Mom."

Her face crinkled into a smile. "David!" His mom, Elisa Landi, was still a beauty with her delicate features and rich auburn hair, despite the few lines of worry that now graced her face. David was sure he'd put them there when he left for the Army. His mom gave him a fierce hug and then held him away from her. "Let me look at you. I've missed you." Her eyes brimmed with unshed tears.

"I've missed you too, Mom," David said. "Don't cry."

His mom gave a tremulous laugh. "Who said I was going to cry?" She blinked a couple of times. "Something must have gotten in my eye."

David smiled. "It's good to see you. Where's Dad?"

"I'm right here." David looked to his left to see his father, Andrea Landi, making his way across the living room to where he stood. The older version of David, he had a mild limp which was only noticeable to those who had known him before the stroke.

"Hi, Dad."

"Good to see you, son. Don't smother him, Elisa."

His mom humphed and walked over to the custom-sized brown leather couch and sat down. "I can do whatever I like."

David chuckled as his father sat next to his mom. It was good to know his parents were still the same. And they looked great together: his mom wore a purple cowl-neck linen dress while his father wore a pink button-down shirt with tan slacks.

"So what did you bring for your lovely mother?" she asked.

David grinned. He'd never seen anyone who loved receiving gifts as much as his mom. It wasn't about how expensive it was; the thought was what counted as far as she was concerned. "Let me get it."

He walked over to where his hand luggage stood, laid it flat on the ground, and opened it. He quickly shut it as his ears grew warm. What did he just see? How had he ended up with feminine lingerie of different colors?

"Is everything okay?" his mom asked.

"Uhm … I think I might have left the gifts in another bag." Did he pick up the wrong bag from the overhead bin? But his had been the only bag in that specific first-class storage space.

"Did you forget any bags at the airport?" his dad asked.

"No. I think it's in one of the bras … sorry … bags that will arrive tomorrow." What was wrong with him? It was like he was tongue-tied.

His mom leaned forward. "What is that?"

David followed her pointed finger to see a pink strap peeking out on the side. Shoot! He quickly tucked it in and zipped up the bag. "It's nothing important." But he felt hot for some reason.

"David, are you alright?" his mom asked. "You are sweating."

David pulled his monogrammed handkerchief from his pocket and wiped his forehead. "I'm fine. Don't worry, I'll make sure I get the gifts to you." Phew. This would have been the embarrassment of the century. He would never have lived it down if his mother had seen the lingerie.

His forehead creased into a frown. But who did the bag belong to? He couldn't imagine how his bag got switched except … Right! It could only belong to the young lady he'd bumped into. Their hand luggages had been the same make and color! He'd just assumed the bag at the bottom of the pile was hers and had taken the wrong one. Now he knew who the owner was, he'd figure out later how to get it back to her and regain his.

David walked back to where his parents sat and slouched into the chair opposite theirs. "How are you guys doing?" he asked.

"We are good. Same as always," his mom responded. "We were more worried with you being on the other side of the world. But I'm grateful to God you are finally home. How are you really doing?" His mom's eyes looked him over.

"I'm doing much better."

His mom studied him for a few moments and then smiled as if satisfied with what she saw. "Okay, that's good to hear."

David turned to his father. "How are you feeling?"

"You mean the stroke? Never been better."

"Don't mind him," his mom said. "His leg is still bothering him. He has weekly physiother-apy, and we're hoping it improves. But I'm just grateful he is still here."

"Oh please, I wasn't going anyway," his dad responded. "No way will I leave you behind. Who would you nag?"

"Andrea!" his mom exclaimed.

David's dad grinned. "Don't worry, I still love you, nagging and all." He turned and gave her a big kiss on the lips.

His mom blushed and smacked his dad's chest. "Andrea, would you stop?"

His father turned to David. "Son, there's nothing like marrying a good woman. Even after all these years, I still love the way your mother calls my name." His dad gave her a look that made her blush. She tickled him. "Okay, okay, love, I'll give it a rest."

David's heart squeezed in pain as he watched them. This was the kind of love that he'd had with Heather, the kind of future he'd wished for with her. One that would never come true now.

His mom cleared her throat. "While we're on the same topic, there's something we need to talk to you about," she said.

David tensed. Same topic? Could this be about marriage? It was too early in the morning to be having this kind of conversation. "Mom, can we eat first? I'm hungry, and if it's a serious talk I'd rather have it on a full stomach," he responded.

"Of course."

Breakfast was delicious as usual. This was the one meal his mom insisted on cooking herself for the family. Lunch and dinner were left for the live-in cook to prepare.

David placed his cutlery on the plate in front of him and waited for his parents to speak.

His father wiped his mouth with a napkin and dropped it on the table. "Wonderful breakfast as always, my beautiful wife," he said to David's mom.

"Why, thank you, dear," his mom said as she blushed.

David chuckled. His father always complimented his mom's cooking without fail. He actually believed his dad did it just to see her blush.

"So have you found a job?" his father asked David.

"Yes, I got an Assistant Professorship spot at Dexington Medical," David responded. "I'll be starting work on Monday."

His parents looked at each other and then smiled at him. What was that exchange all about? It was like they knew something he didn't.

"That's awesome!" his mom said. "Hopefully, we'll see more of you since you'll be working in town."

His father took a sip of water and leaned

back into his seat. "David, as you know, business had been good for us this past year."

That was an understatement—it had been excellent, turning the company into a multi-billion-dollar corporation.

"To give back, we made the decision to start a venture that focused on creating silicone underwires for women that have had reconstructive breast surgery, given your interests and some of the customer feedback we've received," his dad continued. "But we wanted to be more involved in the final product. So, the management team agreed to look for a lingerie company that we could partner with. IntimiRose, a local brand and family-owned business, came to our attention."

Where had he heard that name? David tapped his fingers on his thigh. The name struck a chord with him, but he couldn't recall why.

"The more we looked into them, the more we discovered that the company's vision, products, and culture are a good fit for us. It made more business sense to acquired them instead, but under a separate brand," his dad continued. "They were interested in what we had to offer but wanted to be able to keep the business in the family—it has been handed down for many generations. Neither of us wanted to let go of the opportunity, and an option surfaced as we discussed. We were not a hundred percent sure it would work, but given how much we want this, we figured we had nothing to lose if we explored it."

David was beginning to get a weird vibe about this. Like it had something to do with him personally. "And what was this option?"

"For you and their only daughter to get married."

David froze. "What?" This must be some kind of joke. They couldn't be serious about this.

"I know it sounds strange in this day and age to talk about an arranged marriage," his mom chimed in. "But when I found out who their daughter was, I figured it was worth a shot."

His mother must be kidding. It didn't matter who the girl was. There was no way he was getting married, especially to someone he barely knew. But his curiosity was piqued. Who was this girl that could make his mom, the great advocate for all things love, change her mind? "And who is this young lady?"

His mom gave his dad a look before responding. "Jasmine Banks," she said.

David stiffened. It had been a long time since he'd heard that name, but all the memories associated with it came flooding back. His chest tightened like a boulder had landed on it. He forced himself to take a deep breath. "Jasmine Banks? The same one from high school?"

"Yes," she said.

David couldn't help but laugh. His parents had finally lost their marbles.

There was no way he would marry Jasmine Banks, not even if they tied him up and dragged him to the altar.

CHAPTER 5

"It's not going to happen. There's no way I'm going to marry Jasmine Banks, not now, not ever," David said. "This—"

His mom raised her hand. "Wait, let me finish. We're not asking you to marry her today. Just spend three weeks and get reacquainted."

"I don't have time for this. I just got back, and the next few weeks are going to be very busy for me. The last thing I need is a relationship, especially with someone I don't want to have anything to do with ever again."

"What if there was a misunderstanding?"

"About what? About the fact that she dumped me?"

"What if that's not the whole story?"

"That's not possible. Besides, I'm not interested." David stood up. He didn't have to stay and listen to this. "I need to go. It's been a long trip, and I'm exhausted. Thanks for the breakfast."

"Hold on, it's only three weeks," his father said. "And you promised you would always help us with whatever we needed for the business. Your mom, your sister, and I have been shouldering the responsibility for the company since you left for the Army. Is going on a date to facilitate a business deal that helps your kind of patients too much to ask?"

"But it's not just a date, is it? Speaking of Gabriella, where is she?" Gabriella was David's sister and only sibling.

"She's not happy that you abandoned her, but don't change the subject. We need your help."

"But not this way. This is the rest of my life we're talking about here."

"Yes, the one you've been avoiding since you lost Heather," his mom said.

The mention of her name was like a stab in his heart, and David collapsed back into his chair. He forced himself to take a deep inhale and exhale.

"I know you miss her, but it's time to move on and let go of the past," his mom continued softly. "I know you loved Heather, but have you ever wondered what drew you to her in the first place? If you didn't notice, she had an uncanny resemblance to Jasmine. That was what struck me the first time you introduced her to us. But she was a wonderful person, and I could see why you fell in love with her. That's why I never said anything."

It hadn't occurred to him, but yes, maybe he just had a type, which was normal for most people. But that was where the similarities had ended. They had been different from each other like night and day. Jasmine had always been a spitfire. Heather had been gentle and more soft-spoken. He'd loved Heather for who she was.

"But she's gone now and it's time to live your life again," his mom continued. "And if you really want a fresh start, you need to resolve all the knots in the past, including the issue you had with Jasmine that forced you to leave." David looked up at his mother in surprise. "Yes, David Antonio Landi, I know she's the reason why you left town instead of taking any college offers in the area."

How did his mom know? He hadn't told anyone why he'd selected UCLA.

"David, are you afraid you could fall for her again?" his mom asked.

Like that would happen. It had not worked out then for a reason. He sighed. There were only a few times in his life he'd seen his easygoing mother so determined on an issue—calling him by his full name was another sign. And she had never given up in each case, if memory served him right. She would just stay on him till he caved in, and that was the last thing he needed. It was only for three weeks, right? It would be over before he knew it. And his mom had confirmed that he didn't have to marry her if it didn't work out, which he expected to be the case. "Alright, I'll do it."

His mom beamed, and his father relaxed. "Awesome," his mom said. "I'll call Jasmine's mom and let her know you're on board."

"Does she know yet? Jasmine, I mean," David asked.

"I assume her parents have told her by now."

"What if she doesn't consent to this?"

"Oh, you don't have to worry. She'll agree alright. Just promise me you'll put in your best effort."

Like that would change anything. "Sure."

David sighed. The next three weeks couldn't go by fast enough.

CHAPTER 6

*D*avid put away the last of his books in his new office at Dexington Medical Center and leaned back on his haunches. He'd planned to move his things over the weekend, but the visit with his parents had forced a change in plans.

He'd arrived early Monday morning instead to settle in before the workday started. Luckily he'd only had his reference books, his personal supply of medical equipment, and a big box containing all his research materials to move in. He'd already hung copies of his certificates and state license on the wall. He'd even gone through the on-boarding package his new secretary had left for him, which included his IT credentials.

David was excited to jump back into reconstructive microsurgery again, though working with wounded soldiers had been worthwhile and fulfilling. And he'd been lucky to end up in an office where he had enough space to spread out. He'd been assigned a corner office that showcased a fantastic view of Dexington downtown. David looked around the office appreciatively. It was the kind of office that was reserved for more senior professors, but who was he to complain? He would enjoy it as long as he had the opportunity to do so.

He rose from the floor and stood by the windows, watching as shards of sunlight pierced through the clouds to illuminate a sky otherwise awash with various shades of blue and grey.

Thoughts of what had happened at his parents' house flashed through his mind. He still couldn't believe they had insisted on the arranged dates with Jasmine of all people—they weren't the type to put up appearances.

He shook his head. He would not dwell on this. He had a lot of to-dos on his calendar today, including making sure to drop off the mixed-up hand luggage. The young lady might already be looking for her stuff. He'd examined her luggage tag, but there had been no information on it. He would have taken the bag to the airport's customer service counter yesterday, but he'd gone out-of-town for an appointment and had returned late last night. He hoped he would get back his bag as well. Good thing he had packed all his important stuff in his army duffle bag.

He stepped away from the window and packed away the now empty boxes above the tall cabinet hidden behind the door. He would get his new secretary to dispose of them once she arrived.

A knock sounded, and David looked up. His door opened and a stocky middle-aged man with a receding hairline stepped in. David recognized him from his picture on the hospital website as Prof. Crouch, the Chair of Plastic Surgery who had hired him.

Prof. Crouch smiled and extended a veiny hand for David to shake. "Welcome to the team, Dr. Landi." He looked around. "Nice office."

David stepped forward and took his hand.

"Thank you for having me here, Prof. Crouch. And thanks for the office too."

"It's our pleasure. It was the last one to get renovated on this floor and was just ready this last weekend. May I?" He motioned to the black couch in the office.

David nodded. "Please." Now it made sense why such a good office space had been available. Prof. Crouch sat down, and David did the same.

"So how does it feel to be back in the area?" Prof. Crouch asked. "It must be very different from Germany."

"It's nice to see the family again," David said.

"Did I mention that your father and I were classmates in college?" Noting the surprised look on David's face, he continued, "And no, that's not why you got the position, though being a native of Dexington definitely helped. You were the most qualified of all the surgeons we interviewed, and Professor Pointe had only glowing recommendations for you. I've worked with him for many years and I trust his judgement." Prof. Pointe had been David's department chair at UCLA during his residency and fellowship programs.

"Thank you," David said.

"Okay, I'll get straight to the point since we both have busy days ahead of us. There is an opportunity to submit a proposal to win NIH funding for a one year of research on the long-term effects of reconstructive surgery on hereditary breast cancer management. Winning the grant could work in your favor regarding a professorial position here.

"Professor Tisha Morgan of Gynecologic Oncology will be spearheading the research, and we would like you to be her co-investigator. She's a superstar here at the hospital and someone you would enjoy working with. A couple other doctors from other specialties may end up being involved as well once the financing comes through but only in a supporting role. I'm assuming this is something you would be interested in."

"Absolutely." This was right up David's alley and would allow him to hit the ground running.

"I figured you would be, so I gave Prof. Morgan your office number. She should be reaching out to you any moment now."

"Sounds good."

"Fantastic. Let me know if you need anything. I just wanted to drop by quickly before your day starts." Prof. Crouch stood up.

David got up as well. "Thank you for the warm welcome."

"My pleasure. There should be a dinner tomorrow to meet with the rest of the doctors in the department. Your secretary will give you the details."

"Got it. I'll be there."

"Good to see you, Dr. Landi." With that, Prof. Crouch left David's office.

David leaned against his mahogany desk. It was great to have met Prof. Crouch in person. And the proposal sounded interesting. He was sure he could still write a good one, though his skills were probably rusty.

The phone on his desk rang and he picked it up. "This is Dr. Landi."

"Good morning, Dr. Landi," a crisp female voice said from the other end of the line. "This is Betsy Lane from Prof. Tisha Morgan's office. Is this a good time?"

Just like Prof. Crouch had predicted. "Yes," David responded.

"Prof. Morgan would like to know if you would be available at one p.m. this afternoon for a meeting to discuss the NIH proposal."

David checked his calendar on his cellphone. He was free at that time and would be finished with all required HR paperwork. "Yes, one p.m. is fine," he said.

"Great. The meeting would be in Conference Room 6B North."

"Tell Professor Morgan I'll be there."

"I will. Have a great day, Dr. Landi."

"Thank you." David replaced the phone on its receiver.

He checked his watch. He still had an hour before his meeting with the HR Director. No time like the present to get a head start on his to-dos for the day if he wanted to leave work on time to head to the airport.

He had a mixed-up bag to deliver.

CHAPTER 7

The rest of the weekend had been both busy and unsettling for Jasmine. She'd worked hard to keep her mind away from the lump and the arranged date with Tony, focusing instead on prepping for her new rotation. Jasmine had already been assigned her patients over the weekend and had planned to hit the ground running.

She'd arrived early at the inpatient ward to take over from the night float team, had reviewed the new admits, and had written up orders and discharge notes for her team to take care of. Then she'd walked over with her attending to pre-op to say hello to the OR patients for the day, address their questions, and make sure all necessary paperwork had been signed. Finally, she'd called her gynecologist to tell her about the lump and had then scheduled an appointment for Wednesday at the breast clinic.

Jasmine exited the elevators and walked down the hallway to Conference Room 6B North. She'd just finished her second surgery for the day when she'd received a call from Prof. Trisha Morgan to meet her there. Prof. Morgan was both her mentor and the head of Gynecologic Oncology service, Jasmine's current rotation. She opened the door to see Prof. Morgan already seated at the conference table in the white-walled room, typing away furiously on her laptop. The smell of green tea hung low in the air. She looked up as Jasmine entered and gave her a warm smile.

Prof. Trisha Morgan was a successful gynecologist in high demand in the Dexington area. Tall and graceful with her dread-locked hair in a bun, Prof. Morgan reminded Jasmine of an African princess. With Prof. Morgan's warmth and genuine love for her patients, Jasmine hoped she could someday be as good as she was.

"Hi, Jasmine. Welcome back," Prof Morgan said. "Feel free to grab any seat you like. How was New York?"

Jasmine pulled back a chair and sat down. "It was great and I had fun. Lots of new designs," she responded.

Prof. Morgan shut her laptop and leaned back. "Did you see any dress you personally liked?"

"You mean like for my wedding? Why would I? I'm not planning to get married."

"That's the same thing I said, and here we are. I'm married to the best man in the world, and I have an unexpected but totally welcomed baby on the way." She leaned forward. "And that's why I needed to see you."

"What's going on?"

"My doctor has ordered bed rest. I had a second set of pre-term contractions yesterday which they managed to stop. But this baby isn't supposed to come anytime soon, and they're worried it might be difficult to stop if it happens again. I need to cut back on my workload, which is where I need your help."

"You know I'll assist in any way I can."

"I have this new NIH proposal I just started

working on that focuses on long term effects of reconstructive surgery on hereditary breast cancer management. There is a lot of interest in the research, and I'm hopeful that we can win it if we apply. I'd like you to join the team as the third investigator. I think you would be a good fit given your passion for hereditary gynecologic cancers. I would still be involved, but I intend to take a more hands-off approach. It would also look good for your résumé when you apply for next year's fellowship, which I assume you still want."

"Yes, I do."

"Great."

"But who is the second investigator?"

Prof. Morgan looked at her watch. "He should be joining us shortly."

The conference room door swung open at that precise moment, and a tall young man in a white coat worn over a blue button-down shirt and dark grey pants stepped in.

Jasmine's eyes widened and she gasped.

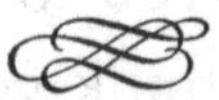

CHAPTER 8

David couldn't believe his eyes. It was the young woman from the airport. What was she doing here? And she was even more stunning than the last time he'd seen her. Who ever thought wearing scrubs could look so sexy?

He forced his eyes away from her to the other woman in the room. Dressed in hospital scrubs, she was beautiful with delicate features and appeared pregnant. She gave him a pleasant smile and extended her hand for a shake.

"Hi, I'm Professor Trisha Morgan. Dr. David Landi, right?"

David shook her hand. The handshake was warm and firm. This was a confident doctor who knew what she was about. "Yes, I'm Dr. Landi. It's nice to meet you."

"Same here." Prof. Morgan motioned to Jasmine. "And this is my resident, Dr. Jasmine Banks. She'll be joining the team."

David froze for a moment before he recovered himself and acknowledged her with a nod. Jasmine Banks? Was she *the* Jasmine Banks? Impossible. The lady standing in front of him was a confident brunette with brown eyes. The other Jasmine Banks was a redhead and proud of it and had striking green eyes. She'd loved fashion and design so much he couldn't imagine her signing up to be a doctor. There had been no light of recognition in her eyes at the mention of his name. She probably only remembered him as the guy from the airport. No way it was the same person. But thank goodness he'd found her. He could return her luggage in exchange for his.

"Please sit," Prof. Morgan said. They all got seated around the conference table. David kept his focus on Prof. Morgan. This was not the time for any distractions.

"Dr. Landi," Prof. Morgan continued. "Thank you for agreeing to work with me. I've heard so much about you from Professor Pointe at UCLA."

"It sounds like a great opportunity."

"It is. I'm excited about it."

David nodded. He was as well. Nothing like working with another rockstar. And he really should call Dr. Pointe and thank him for the recommendations.

Prof. Morgan leaned forward and placed her elbows on the conference table. "However, there've been some changes, which is why I brought Dr. Banks along to this meeting. Unfortunately, I have to step back a bit on this project. I have to be on bed rest for the next few months, so Dr. Banks will be working closely with you instead.

"She and I have worked on some other research proposals together, so she has a good idea of what I like. I believe she even knows more about this subject matter than I do. I'll still work with her in a supervisory role, which I think would give you the best of both worlds. It might take us about two weeks to put together a solid proposal. Would that work for you?"

An opportunity to get closer to this Jasmine Banks? Interesting. He couldn't deny that he didn't mind getting to know her better. And it wasn't as if that meant he had to be in a relationship with her. It would be strictly professional. There was just something about her that he couldn't resist, though he couldn't put his finger on what it was. "Yes, it would. And congratulations on the baby. Is it a boy or a girl?"

"Thank you. We don't know yet. My husband and I want it to be a surprise at birth."

"That's nice too."

Prof. Morgan chuckled. "I know. I hope I can hold off till then. Do you have kids, Dr. Landi?"

David felt a stab in his heart at the question, but he tried not to let it show. He might have had a kid by now if Heather was still alive. Another loss. "No. I'm not married yet."

"Good for you." Prof. Morgan rose slowly to her feet and picked up her laptop. David and Dr. Banks got up as well. "I'm glad we're all agreed. Dr. Landi, it was great meeting you."

"Me too," David said. "Dr. Banks, could you stay for a few minutes? I'd like us to talk through the next steps."

"Sure," Dr. Banks said.

"I'll leave you guys to it. Have a good day."

Prof. Morgan waddled out of the conference room with her laptop under her arm.

"And you too," David said.

The door shut behind her.

And then David and Dr. Banks were the only two in the conference room. The room suddenly felt hot, and David adjusted the collar of his shirt. "I won't take much of your time," he said.

"No worries."

"We meet again. I can't believe you were the lady I bumped into at the airport."

"Right? It's such a small world."

"Did you unpack your luggage by any chance? I opened mine and realized that our luggage may have gotten mixed up." David could feel his ears heating up.

Dr. Banks had a quizzical look on her face. "My luggage?" she asked.

David could see exactly when it dawned on her what that meant. She burst out laughing. "Oh, my goodness! I'm so sorry."

David felt his face grow hot, and he tried to cover it with a cough.

"Are you okay?" she asked with concern.

"I'm fine."

"I'm so sorry. I haven't opened my luggage

since I got back. I had an overnight bag as well and that's where I had most of my things. I hope you weren't too freaked out about it. It must have been embarrassing."

"No, it wasn't." But he could tell his face said otherwise.

David could see she was trying to hide her smile. "Okay. I'll drop off your bag tomorrow at your office. I'm assuming it's on the surgical floor," she said.

"There's no need to hurry." He noticed her arched brow. "I mean …. if it's not convenient for you." He could see her smile was practically begging to be let loose. "Yes, my office is on the surgical floor and tomorrow is fine. I'll leave yours with my secretary. You can drop mine off with her."

"Sounds good."

He grinned. "I'm glad we got that out of the way." Dr. Banks smiled back.

David's heart picked up its pace. He wished he could just take a snapshot of the moment. It was like her whole body came alive with the smile, and it was captivating to watch. Time to change the subject before he did something he would regret. "So back to the proposal. Can we meet at noon on Wednesday? I'll put together my initial thoughts and you can do the same. We'll talk through those then."

"That works for me."

"How about we exchange numbers?" David was asking for work reasons, or that was what he told himself.

The corners of her lips lifted. "Sure." She pulled out her business card from her coat pocket and wrote a number on the back before handing it to him. He did the same and she tucked the card into her pocket. "Anything else?" she asked.

"I think that's it. It was good seeing you again. I'll see you on Wednesday." He extended his hand to her, which she shook. A zap of electricity coursed through him from her touch and made him feel all warm inside. He didn't want to let go of her hand. But he did.

"Have a good rest of the day, Dr. Landi," she said.

CHAPTER 9

Jasmine dried off her hair as she exited the shower. She occupied the master suite on the first floor of the Victorian brownstone apartment she shared with her roommates, Dana and Alicia, who had their own rooms on the second floor. They'd been lucky to rent the apartment at a modest price from Jasmine's aunt.

It was also close to Dexington Medical Center where they all worked—Dana was a fourth-year general surgical resident, while Alicia was a third-year internal medicine resident. As much as Jasmine loved coming home to this place, it was hard to imagine living here without them. But she would have to learn to deal with it since both were engaged and would marry soon.

Jasmine had spent the rest of the day after the meeting with Dr. Landi going back and forth between the wards and the ER to address any inpatient issues and attend to the day's consults. She'd been exhausted by the time she'd signed off, but the quick shower had helped.

She dropped the towel into the laundry basket and sat on her bed as she recalled the day's events. Who would have thought Dr. Landi would be the guy she'd bumped into at the airport? He was even more handsome today without the sunglasses—definitely one of those people who looked good in whatever they wore. She chuckled as she remembered how embarrassed he'd been at mentioning her luggage. His face must have been beet red on seeing the lingerie.

David Landi seemed like a pretty decent guy from what she'd seen so far. She couldn't deny she felt a ripple of excitement at the thought of working with him, especially on a research topic that was dear to her heart. But meeting him again seemed too coincidental. Was God at work here? Was there hope that something special could happen between them? She wasn't sure. God knew about her health situation, and she didn't think He'd bring someone else into it. Wouldn't that be unfair to the guy? So a relationship just wasn't possible in her life right now.

She pulled her knees up under her chin. But the main shocker had been that his name was David Landi. Who would have thought? She'd always assumed the Landi surname was uncommon. Thank goodness he wasn't Tony Landi. She'd also overheard one of the nurses mention that Dr. Landi had just come back from the Army. That was something Tony would never do—he hadn't been exactly the type who followed strict rules.

She dropped her feet back on the floor. But enough about David Landi. She still had some reading to take care of tonight before she could call it a day. And the upcoming appointment with the breast clinic was always there, hovering at the back of her mind like a cobweb that couldn't be swept away.

A knock sounded on her door, and Jasmine looked up. Dana, a petite beauty with blonde hair and gorgeous blue eyes, poked her head into the room. "Hey, you," she said.

Jasmine smiled and patted the bed space beside her. "When did you get back?" Dana and her fiancé, Josh Roman, had taken a quick trip to London for the weekend to watch the football team he co-owned play a match.

Dana entered the room and flopped on the bed. "This morning. You were gone by the time I got in."

"Did you have fun?"

Dana's face took on a dreamy look. "Yes! We sat in the owner's box, which was very different from being in the stands. His team won, so that was awesome. We then spent Sunday sightseeing. The weather was a bit warmer than here which was nice, and Josh was an absolute gentleman as always. Did you have fun in New York?"

"I saw some cool bridal designs and took some pictures. Do you want me to show you? It might give you some wedding dress ideas."

Dana collapsed back on the bed. "Ugh!" She turned her head to look at Jasmine. "Would I be a bad bride if I said I'm not looking forward to the whole wedding planning thingy? I always thought I'd love it since I like fashion a lot, but seeing Alicia actually go through it has changed my mind on things. So-o-o many details. My work schedule is already crazy enough as it is, especially with the last-minute change to focus on pediatric surgery instead of vascular surgery like I'd always planned."

Jasmine looked down at Dana. "You could always hire a wedding planner like Alicia did."

"Her woman is great, but I don't think we'd really mesh well. Hey, how about you plan my wedding? You already know the kinds of things I like."

Jasmine gave her a bemused look. "You're kidding, right?"

Dana laughed. "Just joking. Your schedule is probably as bad as mine. I have this weird feeling you might be in an obstetrics rotation by the time my wedding rolls around, and you know what that means. Those babies screaming their way into the world would be the ones determining your schedule."

Jasmine laid a hand on Dana's shoulder. "Don't worry, I'll be there. I'll probably take a vacation. Have you decided on a date?"

Dana let out a sigh. "Not yet. It's hard figuring out what I want. Don't look at me like that. That wedding scrapbook I put together over the years is not helping. And who knew I'd be marrying a billionaire and have all these expectations I now have to meet? Josh says he's fine with whatever I want, but guys don't get it. Once they have their tuxedo, they're all set. He seems to have forgotten his father is a renowned orthopedic surgeon, and all these doctors from all over the country and even some from overseas will be coming for the wedding. It's a lot more pressure than I imagined."

Jasmine thought for a moment. She had spoken to her aunt over the phone last week and she'd mentioned she was feeling the itch to plan an event. "What if I ask my aunt to help?"

Dana sat up. "Are you serious? *The* Rebecca Scott, planner extraordinaire for the celeb weddings I've always admired in magazines, being in charge of my wedding? That would be a dream come true!"

Jasmine grinned. "Okay, I'll give her a call. I'm almost sure she'll agree to do it."

Dana squealed and gave Jasmine a hug. "Thank you! You have no idea what you've done. I can finally breathe."

"Happy to help."

Dana loosened her grip and held Jasmine

away from her. She searched Jasmine's face. "But you look tired. Is everything okay?"

Trust Dana to notice. Jasmine gave her a weak smile. "I'm fine. I'm still recovering from the trip that's all."

Jasmine could tell Dana didn't really believe her, but she didn't push further. "If you say so. But you know you can talk to me about anything, right? You're like the sister I never had."

"Sure, I know that. But I'm fine."

"Okay, I'll let you rest." Dana got up. "Hey, you're not wearing the wig."

"We never agreed I would wear it at night. They are called wigs for a reason."

"I wish I had gotten you to wear it much longer. And short hair fits you. You should try it sometime."

Jasmine made a face. "In your dreams. I can't wait for this to be over on Friday. I hate how my scalp gets itchy under it. I admit the length isn't so bad. I'll be careful not to fall into your trap next time."

Dana laughed. "Let's hope that's possible."

"Oh, yes it is. Anyway, I'll let you know what my aunt says."

Dana gave her an okay sign. "Thanks again. Goodnight."

"Goodnight."

Dana left the room and shut the door behind her.

Jasmine let out a sigh and laid back on the bed. She didn't like keeping secrets from Dana, but there was no way she was going to put a dark cloud over what could be the happiest day of Dana's life. After what Dana had been through, she deserved her once-in-a-lifetime dream wedding.

But thinking about the wedding reminded her she might never get a chance of a wedding of her own. She'd thought she'd be okay without it. But seeing Dana and Alicia in love had changed her. And meeting David Landi had sparked something in her which refused to die down. But the lump and the possibility of cancer clouded everything.

A sense of emptiness filled Jasmine. *Please, God, I need You.* Wednesday could well be the beginning of the end for her. And the worst thing was there was nothing she could do about it. She could only keep busy and not dwell on it.

Wednesday would be here soon enough.

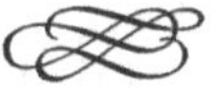

CHAPTER 10

*D*avid closed his eyes as he reclined in the poolside chair. He'd activated the automatic roofing system which helped trap in the warmth of his apartment's heated penthouse swimming pool. He'd loved to relax here in the evenings whenever he was in town from Los Angeles, and that feeling had not changed.

The rest of his day had been busy but rewarding. He'd finished all HR paperwork, completed the on-boarding process and hospital orientation, met a couple of his colleagues informally, familiarized himself with both his surgical team and the team of medical residents he would supervise, and met his first patients. His secretary had made sure any outstanding IT inventory was delivered. He still had dinner with other surgeons in his department scheduled for tomorrow, but he was well on his way to getting embedded into the system. And he hadn't needed to go to the airport. He'd completed almost everything he'd scheduled for the day except one: reaching his sister, Gabriella.

They had always been close, but his move to Germany and the Army had put some distance between them. He'd tried her number over the weekend, but it had gone straight to voicemail. He was sure she'd listened to it, which meant only one thing: she was very upset with him. And it was all his fault. After Heather's loss, he'd picked up the phone multiple times to call her while in Germany but had held back. Gabriella's personality had been so similar to Heather's that he'd been afraid he'd break down at the sound of her voice. So he'd withdrawn instead, and their relationship had paid the price. Now, he had to try his best to mend the rift between them.

He opened his eyes, picked up his phone from the poolside table, and dialed her number. She answered at the second ring.

"Hi Ella," he said. Ella had been his nickname for her since childhood.

"What do you want?" she said in a businesslike tone. Which she only used for strangers. He was in serious trouble.

"I'm sorry."

The line went silent for a while. Only the sound of her breathing indicated she was still there.

"I'm sorry, Ella," David repeated quietly.

"You hurt me, David."

"I'm sorry. It was wrong of me."

"I know losing Heather broke you, but I lost you too. You were my best friend, the brother I looked up to. It was like I didn't matter anymore."

"It's all my fault. Please forgive me."

She let out a sigh. "I've missed my big brother."

"I've missed you too, twinkie."

She laughed. "Don't call me that."

David let out a sigh of relief. She'd forgiven him, though he probably still had some ways to go to get back into her good graces. But he would do whatever it took.

He settled back into his chair. "How are you doing?"

"I'm good. Just very busy. See what you did to me, David? I practically have no life. And Dad's stroke made it worse."

"Is there anything I can do to make it better? Do you want me to hire some help?"

"I can hire my own help, thank you. Hey, I have a good idea. Why don't I send you all the departmental quarterly reports, and you read and summarize each one for me?"

David groaned inwardly. Everyone hated those reports since they ran several hundred pages long, though they were necessary. She really got him this time. But he would do it if it meant everything could be well between them. "Alright, send them over."

"Awesome!" She yawned.

"Where are you?" he asked.

"I'm still at the office."

"At this hour? It's very late."

"I know, but what can I do? There is so much to get done."

"Promise me you'll cut back a little. I don't want anything happening to you too."

"Okay, I promise." She yawned again. "Don't

worry, I'm leaving in about ten minutes."

"Okay, I'll let you go. Love you, Sis."

"Hold on. I met Jasmine Banks in New York. Remember her?"

Had his parents told her about the date? That was one conversation topic he had no plans to revisit. "Ella, can we not talk about this?"

"Alright. Goodnight."

"Goodnight." The line went dead.

David blew out a breath. He'd messed up big time, but she'd forgiven him. *Thank you, God.* It had been good hearing her voice again.

He yawned. It was time to go to bed. He had a full day tomorrow with surgery in the morning, clinic in the afternoon, and dinner with his department peers in the evening. And then he had the meeting with Jasmine on Wednesday.

His lips turned up in a smile. He still couldn't believe Dr. Banks was the lady from the airport. He hadn't expected her to be a doctor, but he was relieved she was in a different specialty, which eliminated any ethics issues if they dated. Now why was that thought popping into his head when he had no plans for a relationship? *Get it together, David.*

But it had been good to see her again. Sure,

he'd been embarrassed about bringing up her luggage, but hearing her laugh had done strange things to his insides and touched a part of him that he'd thought dead since Heather's passing. And the sparks had been there again when he'd shaken her hand. But who was he kidding? Maybe he felt that way since she was the first young lady he'd interacted with since he came back. Yes, that was probably it.

But he had to admit he'd been a bit disappointed that she was only a resident—he'd been expecting to work with an attending on the research proposal. He wasn't sure how much she could bring to the table despite the vote of confidence Prof. Morgan had given her.

He couldn't deny that a part of him was looking forward to working with her and getting to know her better. But that was all it could be. The research paper was too important to his future to mess up with any distractions, even if it was from a beautiful doctor who liked to tuck her hair behind her ear. And yes, he had noticed. It wasn't such a big deal if he had, right?

But nothing else could come from their

working together. He wasn't looking for anyone to replace Heather.

He had to stay super focused. That was all that mattered now.

Their meeting on Wednesday would be strictly professional. Right?

CHAPTER 11

Jasmine resisted the urge to rub the area where the needle from the biopsy had pierced. It still ached a little, though she was sure the pain would go away soon.

Wednesday had dawned, and she'd greeted it with both enthusiasm and trepidation. Jasmine had arrived at the breast clinic for the appointment, met with Dr. Allen—the surgeon who was going to handle her case—and had a breast examination. Dr. Allen had confirmed the presence of the lump and had requested an MRI and a needle biopsy for it. The tissue sample from the biopsy had been sent to the pathology lab, and she expected to hear back about the results within the next seventy-two hours.

They were going to be the longest hours of her life. The challenge was remaining focused till the results came out. Staying busy by taking care of her patients had helped, but it was hard to stop her thoughts from running rampant at times like this, when all she was doing was waiting in the conference room for Dr. Landi to arrive. He'd called to let her know he was running a few minutes late.

"Sorry about that." Jasmine looked up to see Dr. Landi breeze into the room, his white coat flapping behind him. Was it her imagination or was the room suddenly brighter? It wasn't like he was an angel. Or was he?

She tried to clear her head without shaking it. What was wrong with her? "It's okay," she responded instead.

"I apologize," he said. "I was called in to assist with an emergency surgery and it ran longer than expected."

"It's fine."

Dr. Landi pulled out the chair next to hers and sat down. His citrusy sandalwood scent filled her nostrils, and she resisted the urge to lean in. "How has your week been?" he asked.

"Good. Hectic. Nothing earth shattering."

He chuckled. That cute dimple again. It was truly on a mission to disarm her.

"And yours?" she asked.

He rubbed his brow. "Still working on settling in. I got the bag. Thanks."

"I got mine too. You don't have to worry anymore about the lingerie," she couldn't help teasing him.

His ears turned red, and he adjusted in his seat. "No worries."

Jasmine grinned. This was a good topic for poking fun at him in the future. Now, why was she assuming they'd still be hanging out by then? Hmmm. Not a bad idea if he kept looking as dreamy as he did in his scrubs right now. Reminded her of that TV show—what was it called again?

"Okay, can we get started?" David asked.

She mentally pinched herself. *Focus, Jasmine.* "Of course, yes."

"Good." Then his stomach growled, and he flushed. "Sorry, I haven't had anything to eat today."

This was one thing Jasmine was fastidious about—making sure people around her ate well. She couldn't let him stay like this, and she rose to her feet.

"What are you doing?" Dr. Landi asked, looking up at her.

"I can't let you go hungry."

Dr. Landi beckoned at her to sit down. "It's fine. I'll grab something to eat once we're done." But his abdomen rumbled again.

The corners of Jasmine's mouth lifted in a smile. "I think that stomach needs your attention now. There is a nearby cafe that serves good simple meals. We can grab something to eat and chat about the proposal at the same time. Come on, let's go."

Jasmine placed her hand under her chin as she watched Dr. Landi eat. They sat across each other at a table near the cafe's entrance which had been the only one available. It was one of those little places with tables covered with cheery checkered tablecloths where they served fresh grab-and-go lunch packs. The thick smell of freshly ground coffee, roast beef, chicken soup, and fresh homemade bread saturated the air. Jasmine could hear the distant clatter of utensils coming from the kitchen. None of today's food choices had appealed to her, so she'd settled for a cup of coffee. David had paid for their orders.

She scolded herself at her audacity. What had gotten into her? He was an attending for goodness sake, and she'd ordered him to grab lunch. Good thing he didn't have direct supervision over her, or it would have caused a ruckus in the hospital and maybe backfired in the future.

But it had been the right call. He was practically scarfing down the whole sandwich, though he looked graceful doing it. And he'd ordered a pastrami, just like Tony would have.

Hold on. Why was she thinking of Tony at this time? No, no, no, that was a definite mood killer. True, she wasn't trying to set up some sort of wonderful ambience with Dr. Landi, but still. And look at David! Now, this was a man she wouldn't have minded going on an arranged date with. If nothing else, she could feast her eyes on him. What a glorious way to pass the evening!

Soon David was done with the meal and he wiped his mouth with the napkin.

Jasmine looked down and took a sip of her coffee. Good thing he hadn't caught her staring like she was a fangirl or something.

"I needed this," he said. "Thanks."

"Glad to help," Jasmine replied.

David pulled out his tablet from his coat pocket and swiped its surface. She guessed he was searching for something and assumed he'd found whatever it was, because he placed the tablet on the table and leaned back into his chair. "Okay, let's talk about the proposal in the few minutes we have left. Dr. Morgan sent me the initial shell she's put together. I'm assuming you've seen it."

"Yes, I have a copy."

"Great. I took a look at it, and I'm good with the sections she had outlined. The content, however, is what is more crucial. She's included her initial thoughts, but I think it still needs to be really fleshed out. Are there any specific sections you feel more comfortable taking?"

"No, I'm fine with any of them."

He looked at the surface of his tablet. "Why don't I handle sections A, B, D, and G and you take Sections C, E, and F? We can talk through each one to make sure we're in sync once we have a first draft in place. Does that work for you?" He looked up at her.

"Yes, I'm good with those."

"Awesome. When do you think you can pull something together? We'd probably need to meet soon to review what we have, given the tight deadline."

Jasmine pulled up her calendar on her phone. "How about four p.m. on Friday?"

Dr. Landi checked his schedule. "I have a meeting at that time and an appointment after."

"I'm unavailable much later that evening as well. I have an appointment too."

He scanned his calendar. "How about Tuesday?"

"Same time?"

"We could do that. Maybe grab lunch together like this?"

Ah, a man after her heart. Of course, lunch would be fantastic. "I'm fine with that," she said.

"Good. I'm sorry I have to rush off. I know this is our first time working together, and it would have been nice to get to know more about you beyond just the proposal."

Oh, she would like that. She would like that very much. "No worries. We've still got time before the proposal is done."

"Awesome." He got up and picked up his tablet and his trash. Thanks again for the lunch. Are you ready to leave now?"

"No, I'll just stay a few minutes and finish my coffee."

"Okay. Have a good rest of the day. See you soon."

She smiled at him and watched as he left the cafe.

Jasmine liked the sound of that.

She really did.

CHAPTER 12

The sound of the doorbell chimed through the whole apartment. Jasmine had just finished cleaning the refrigerator, and she wiped her hands with the kitchen towel before she went to get the door.

But Dana beat her to it. "I'll get it," she said as she walked to door dressed in a short yellow frock.

Jasmine had been looking forward to her regular Thursday evening hangout with Dana and Alicia. They led such busy lives that it was sometimes hard to see each other during the week. It had even gotten worse after Alicia had moved out partially and found another apartment that was closer to her niece-turned-daughter's school. Willow had spent most of her life living in the hospital as a cystic fibrosis patient but had become well enough to be able to attend school after some radical treatment.

Jasmine had decided she wouldn't tell them about the lump. But she believed the time spent catching up with them would help relieve some of her stress about it.

She walked into the living room just as Alicia entered the apartment. The space shared an open concept floor plan with the dining area and kitchen, and boasted grand bay windows, a fireplace, crown molding, and a winding staircase that led to the upper floors.

"Hey, you," Jasmine said. 'Where's Willow?"

Alicia, a slim dark-haired beauty, dropped her bag on the coffee table, and flopped on the couch. Even clad in cashmere sweater and jeans with legs that went on for miles, she still looked stunning. No wonder Blake, her fiancé, had fallen for her.

"She has a sleepover with Blake's mom," Alicia said. "I dropped her off on my way here." Sarah Dexington, Blake's mom had already claimed Willow as her grandchild even though

Blake and Alicia were not yet married, and Willow adored her in return.

"Speaking of sleepovers, is the wedding dress slumber party still happening next Saturday?" Dana asked from the chair she'd claimed across from Alicia. Given how crazy their schedules were, Alicia had arranged to have her wedding planner fly over to Italy and bring back loads of wedding dresses for Alicia to try on. They'd decided to turn it into a slumber party, and Blake's mom had offered to host it.

"Yep," Alicia said. "I'm so excited just thinking about it. Good thing none of us are on call that weekend. It still feels surreal that I'm getting married soon."

Jasmine smiled. If anyone deserved true love, it was Alicia. She'd made mistakes in the past but had survived through them and worked hard to make sure Willow got all the medical care, treatment, and love she'd needed while still juggling a busy residency schedule. And then she'd met Blake, who loved her flaws and all.

"Who else is coming, apart from Willow, Blake's mom, and us?" Jasmine asked as she sat cross-legged on the floor in her normal yoga outfit and leaned against the coffee table.

"Mrs. Dexington Senior, Blake's grandmother," Alicia answered.

Dana sat up. "She's in town?" Blake's grandma now spent most of her year traveling around the world and only came back to Dexington for short periods of time. "I heard she is a hoot from what Josh told me."

"Yeah. Blake told me my party just got more interesting if Grandma is going to be there."

Jasmine chuckled. "I can't wait to meet her. So we probably don't need our regular Thursday girls' hangout next week, right?"

"No, we don't," Alicia said. She turned to Dana. "So what's going on with your planning? It can't be easy prepping for a wedding involving Professor Roman."

"You know what? He's not so bad," Dana said. "Things have gotten much better since he accepted our relationship, and you can tell he's super proud of me. And his mom is an angel. She offered to help with the wedding, but she's had a prior commitment for this new NGO that she's helping get off the ground, and I know she's stretched thin. I was worried for a while, but everything is fine now. Jasmine's aunt has agreed to plan my wedding for me!"

"That's wonderful!" Alicia said.

"I know. I'm so excited just thinking about it. Thanks again, Jasmine."

"You're welcome," Jasmine said with a grin.

"Have you guys met?" Alicia asked.

"Not yet," Dana said. "Her aunt is going to be back in town starting next week. I can't wait."

It was time to tell them what was going on. "Girls, I have news." Two pairs of eyes focused on Jasmine. "I have an arranged-marriage date tomorrow."

The room was silent for a few moments. One could hear a pin drop.

"What?" Jasmine asked, looking from Alicia to Dana.

"I can't believe this," Dana said.

"Neither can I," Alicia chimed.

"Guys, what's going on?" Jasmine asked.

"Jasmine, you never go on dates. Like this is the miracle of the century," Alicia said. "Hallelujah!"

"Who is he? What does he do? How did he get you to agree?" Dana asked as she moved closer to the edge of her seat. "Spill."

"Wait, one question at a time," Jasmine said. "It's not what you guys think."

"An arranged-marriage date? Isn't that just a blind date?" Dana asked.

"It's a little more than that. Our parents want us to get married but have conceded to giving us three weeks to see if we are ready to commit."

"Three weeks. That's super short to know if he is the one," Dana said.

"But didn't it take you less than that?" Alicia asked. "Mine did."

"Yeah, but there was no pressure of an immediate marriage hanging over our heads. I was only supposed to be engaged with Josh. This is more intense." Dana had been fake engaged to Josh before they finally fell in love.

"What's with that look on your face?" Alicia asked as her soft brown eyes searched Jasmine's. "You don't seem too keen on it. Is he someone you know?"

Jasmine then told them about the conversation that had transpired between her and her parents, and how Tony Landi was the guy who'd failed her when she needed him most.

Dana's mouth hung open by the time she

was done. "Unbelievable. What a jerk!" she finally said. "How could they arrange a date with someone like that?"

"My mom keeps insisting that there is a misunderstanding," Jasmine said.

"Do you think that's possible?" Alicia asked.

"No, I don't believe it," Jasmine said. "You should have seen the way he looked at me then, like he believed I was the class slut."

Alicia got down on her knees and gave her a hug. Dana's arms soon encircled her too. "I'm so sorry. This must be hard for you."

Jasmine took a deep breath and exhaled. This was what she'd needed. She'd known Alicia and Dana would understand. "Thanks, guys. I'll be fine. It's just three weeks, and then he'll be gone from my life."

"Do you know what he does now?" Alicia asked.

"No idea. Probably works at his parents' company," Jasmine responded.

"He is so lucky I'm on call tomorrow. I would have gone to your date and told him what I thought about him. No one messes with my sister," Dana said with an angry look on her face.

Jasmine couldn't have been prouder of her. Dana was usually the quiet one, so it was interesting to see her all worked up.

Jasmine gave her a hug. "Thank you for even thinking about it."

"I hope you go and give him a piece of your mind," Dana said.

"I have a different opinion about it," Alicia said. "I think you should use this date to address any unresolved issues from the past and find out why he disappeared. You deserve to know. It might be difficult, but try to keep an open mind and hear him out."

"The ball is in your court, Jasmine," Dana said. "But more importantly, have you picked out what you're going to wear?"

"I plan to wear whatever I have in my wardrobe," Jasmine replied.

"No no no," Dana said with a shake of her index finger. "You have to wear a killer outfit to show him what he missed out on by bailing on you."

"I don't know. I'll think about it," Jasmine said.

"Okay, but let us know how it goes," Alicia

said. "Don't hesitate to call me if you need anything." She stood up. "I have to go."

"Why?" Dana asked. "We've still got time."

"I know. I have a date with Blake. The poor guy is practically drowning under work, what with taking over leadership of the hospital and staying on top of his residency commitments. He just needs to get away for a little while, and this is the one night we both seem to have some time available. But I told him I'd only meet him after I'd spent some time with you ladies."

"Where are you guys going?" Dana asked.

Alicia picked up her bag from the coffee table. "I have no idea; it's supposed to be a surprise. I still need to go home and change. I'll see you guys later. Jasmine, I'll be waiting for your call to hear how everything went." She walked to the door.

"Bye," Jasmine said. She would try and keep an open mind at tomorrow's date, like Alicia had suggested.

But there was no way she was going to buy a new dress.

Tony Landi wasn't worth it.

CHAPTER 13

Jasmine looked around the hotel lobby as she stood outside the entrance of the hotel's ground floor restaurant. The place was teeming with people either standing and talking in groups, sitting in the designated areas around the massive lobby, or waiting to be attended to by the hotel's concierge.

She straightened her outfit—a high-necked cream coat dress, paired with nude pumps, that showed off her glorious red hair held up in a slick ponytail. She'd missed her hair. Thank goodness the brunette wig dare with Dana was over.

She wasn't supposed to be nervous, but she

was. She hadn't seen Tony Landi in many years. Was he still the lanky guy with full hair she'd known? She hoped he was bald and fat—that was what he deserved after the way he'd treated her.

The memories came flooding back. She could remember it like it had been yesterday. She'd gotten a note in class saying that Tony Landi wanted to meet her in their special place after school. She'd wondered why the note hadn't come through Gabriella, Tony's sister, who had been their go-between, but she'd just assumed it was urgent, which was why he'd given it to a girl in tenth grade who she barely knew. Jasmine had been in eleventh grade at the time, while Tony had been in twelfth.

She'd practically skipped to the place and waited, but Tony didn't come. As she'd been about to leave, Ken Foster, a big bully in her class who she'd learned to ignore after he'd hit on her a couple of times, showed up. It turned out he'd been the one to send the note. He'd forced a kiss on her and tried to rape her, but she'd managed to hit him in the crotch and run away. She'd been afraid to report him because Ken's father had been an Assistant District

Attorney at the time, and it would have been a case of he-said-she-said.

But that had been a mistake, because she'd arrived at school the next day to rumors and whispers. Her classmates had steered away from her like she had a disease and she'd wondered why. And then she'd seen the monster bragging to Tony in the hallway how Jasmine was such a slut.

But what had killed her had been the look in Tony's eyes when he'd seen her. Fury, disappointment, hurt, like he'd believed it. Jasmine had known that it was over in that moment. She'd fled home and locked herself up in her room.

She'd later heard Tony had some altercation with the creep, but it had been too late. The damage was done, and she'd been a mess for the next few weeks. Then she'd heard Tony had left town. Just like that. He hadn't even bothered to look for her or leave her a note.

Then everything had gotten worse. Jasmine had found out about the BRCA gene mutation she carried, and then her grandmother had passed away. Her parents became so worried about her that they pulled her from school and sent her on a trip overseas for a year with her mom, after which she'd returned and was then homeschooled to finish high school and take the SAT. That was when she swore off relationships; they only hurt her, and her cancer risk further reduced her chances of having a meaningful one.

And now, here she was opening herself up to meet the same person that had hurt her before. Her breath caught in her chest. *Breathe, Jasmine, breathe. He is just like any other guy.*

Jasmine heard someone approaching her and looked up to see the maître d, a short stocky guy in a crisp black suit, standing in front of her.

"Good evening, ma'am," he said. "How may I help you?"

"Table for Tony Landi?"

"This way, please." He turned and led her through the restaurant and toward the back. All the tables they passed were filled—it was Friday night after all.

And then they approached a table set apart from the others in a corner of the restaurant that had dimmed lighting, which gave the space an air of privacy. A young man with dark hair was seated at the table with his head bent over what looked like a journal.

"Here you go, ma'am," the maître d said.

At that moment, the young man looked up.

Jasmine's eyes widened, and she froze.

CHAPTER 14

David tugged at his tie—his mother had insisted that he dress up. Well, this would be the last time he'd wear one for a date. It had been a long time since he'd worn a tie, and it felt like a noose around his neck. But he'd acquiesced since his mom had made the arrangements, and so here he was.

He checked the time. Jasmine Banks was running late. That was a sure sign she wasn't keen on being here as well, just like him. But she had no reason to feel that way—she'd been the one who'd broken his heart. David had arrived on time, though this was the last place he wanted to be. Jasmine should have respected his time as well since she'd agreed to come. He would stick around for a few minutes and then he would leave if she hadn't shown up. He flipped through a medical journal he'd brought along as he waited.

Then he heard voices near his table, and he looked up to see the maître d standing next to a lady with flaming red hair. But the face associated with it was one he knew. How had she known he would be here?

"Dr. Banks! What are you doing here? You look different," he said.

She froze as if in a trance. What was wrong with her? Then he remembered she had mentioned she also had an appointment. Maybe she had a date here too.

"Are you Tony Landi?" she asked in a steel voice.

A sudden coldness hit his core. How did she know his nickname? He'd been called Tony since he was little all through high school, but he'd had to use his first name David for official reasons after the company was launched. He'd gotten used to it and never gone back. It's been a long time since he'd been called Tony, and he was sure he hadn't mentioned it at the hospital.

"How did you know?" he asked. "Tony is the shortened form of my middle name Antonio."

"This is insane." She turned and began to walk away.

David felt a heavy feeling in his stomach. It couldn't be. "Wait!" He got up, raced after her, and grabbed her arm. "What's wrong? What are you doing here? How did you know my name?"

"Let go of me!" Jasmine said.

David could hear the room grow silent as patrons turned their attention at them. He let his hand drop.

Jasmine put a hand on her forehead. "I can't believe this. This must be a dream."

David stood in her way. "Please tell me what is going on," he said quietly. His heart beat so loudly that he was afraid everyone could hear it.

She gave a sound between a cry and a laugh. "I'm Jasmine Banks, your date, the girl you dumped in high school and took off from."

David froze. This couldn't be happening. Dr. Banks was *the* Jasmine Banks? "But you had dark hair."

"It was a wig. Women wear those, remember? Even colored contacts are in vogue." She ran a hand over her hair. "This must be some kind of joke."

And that's when he noticed the twin pools of her familiar green eyes, and the truth hit him like a punch in the stomach. The girl from high school and Dr. Jasmine Banks were one and the same, though the latter was older and more beautiful.

"I can't do this." She pushed past him and headed to the restaurant's exit.

"Jasmine, wait!"

Even though he couldn't believe what had just happened, they had to talk and make sense of everything.

So David chased after her.

CHAPTER 15

Jasmine fought the tears that threatened to run down her face as she hurried through the lobby and then through the hotel's revolving doors. God must be playing a joke on her. If not, why would David Landi be Tony Landi? And here she'd been, daydreaming about the guy who had torn her heart to shreds. What a fool she was. She heard him calling her name, but she ignored him. She had to get away from here as fast as possible.

Her phone rang. Who could be calling her? She didn't really want to speak with anyone right now. But what if it was important? She couldn't allow Tony Landi to mess up her life more than he already had.

She stopped at the curb, pulled her phone from her clutch, and looked at the screen. It was Dr. Allen.

Her heart quickened. She'd thought he wouldn't call until next week when she hadn't heard back from them by the afternoon. *Please, God, let it be good news.*

She took a deep breath and swiped the answer button. "This is Jasmine Banks," she said.

"Good evening, Dr. Banks. This is Dr. Allen. Would it be possible for you to come by my office on Monday, let's say in the afternoon?" he asked in a calm tone over the line.

Her stomach knotted, and she swallowed. This was a telltale sign something was wrong. Might as well hear the news now. If not, she wouldn't be able to sleep this whole weekend. She noticed Tony—or was it David?—from the corner of her eye, standing a few feet away, giving her space. "Please go ahead and tell me the results."

"Is it an appropriate place to talk?"

Jasmine looked around—there were some

folks standing and waiting for their cars and two cabs parked a few feet away. No, it wasn't the ideal location, but it wouldn't make a difference. She had to know. "Yes."

"Do you have someone there with you?"

"I have someone close by." Which was true, though the person in question was her enemy. "Please give it to me straight."

"The pathology results just came out. Unfortunately, I have some bad news. We found some cancerous cells in the tissue sample. I'll need you to come in so we can discuss your treatment options."

Jasmine didn't hear the rest of what Dr. Allen said and her hand dropped down to her side. Cancer. She had cancer. She took a step. The dreaded C word. This was no longer a case of maybe. She had it. What she'd feared most had finally happened to her. Jasmine took another step. How could this night have gotten much worse? She took another step and then another.

"Jasmine, watch out!" She turned at the direction of the voice.

Something solid hit her body.

Then her world went black.

Jasmine woke up to see herself lying on a hospital bed, an antiseptic smell strong in the air. She looked down on herself. Good thing she was still in her clothes. She tried to get up, but her whole body ached all over like she'd been run over by a bus, and an IV line snaked from a stand into her left arm. She looked around. This wasn't Dexington Medical Center. Where was she?

"I see you're awake." Jasmine looked up to see a black buxom nurse wheeling a mobile cart into her cubicle. "What's your name?"

"Jasmine Banks." Even her voice sounded tired to her ears. "Where am I?"

"You are at Tanner Memorial." Wasn't that the small hospital a few feet away from the hotel she'd been at for the arranged date? "What's today's date?"

"Uhm, I can't remember. End of April?"

The nurse checked the level of the bag of IV fluid hanging on Jasmine's left. She scanned Jasmine's patient wristband, compared the ID to what she had on her screen, donned a set of gloves, and converted the IV line to a heparin lock. Now Jasmine was no longer tethered to the IV stand.

"You are lucky to be alive and uninjured," the nurse said. "The young man who saved you had it much worse."

Who had saved her? All she could remember was someone shouting her name and then being hit by something.

The screen around her cubicle parted, and her mom breezed in, looking great as usual in a purple turtleneck sweater and blue jeans. "Thank God you are awake," she said. "You gave us quite a scare. How are you feeling, darling?" She gave Jasmine a hug.

Jasmine winced. "Mom, it hurts."

Her mom relaxed her hold. "Sorry. Where's Tony?"

Why was her mom asking about him? Couldn't she just forget about the arranged-marriage date? "Really, Mom? You are asking about a date while your precious child is in the hospital?"

Her mom gave her a quizzical look. "What do you mean? I should ask about him," her mom said matter-of-factly. "He saved your life."

Jasmine froze. "He did what?"

"The young man is in the cubicle next door," the nurse said as she left.

Jasmine looked at her mom. "What happened?" she asked.

"I heard a car came out of nowhere in front of the hotel and almost collided with you. Tony was able to reach you in time and used his body to shove you out of the way. But he ended up getting hit instead. He was lucid enough to call his mom and tell her what had happened, and his mom called me."

"Is he alright?" She had to know. He'd saved her life even if she wanted nothing to do with him.

"Why don't we head over to the next cubicle and find out?"

Jasmine trudged behind her mom into the next cubicle. David was sitting up in bed, his mom next to him, a couple of pillows behind him, and his right arm in a velcro sling. Otherwise, he looked okay.

Her heart fluttered, and she grew mad at herself. How could she still feel attracted to

David when she'd just found out he was Tony Landi, the guy who had betrayed her?

His mom stood as soon as she saw Jasmine's mom.

"Hello, David," Jasmine's mom said. "How is he doing?" she asked David's mom.

"He's okay, thank God," David's mom replied as she came toward them. That was when she noticed Jasmine. "You must be Jasmine," she said with a smile that was similar to David's.

"Good evening, Mrs. Landi," Jasmine responded.

"Oh, please, *the* Mrs. Landi is dead. Just call me Elisa." She flashed another smile and pulled Jasmine in for a hug.

Jasmine flinched. What was with all the hugs today? Did they forget she'd just been in an accident?

Elisa must have noticed because she let go of Jasmine immediately. "Are you okay?" she asked.

"It hurts a little," Jasmine responded.

"Sorry," Elisa said with genuine remorse.

"So how are you doing?" Jasmine's mom asked David.

"I'm doing much better, Mrs. Banks."

"What's with all the formality? Just call me Leah."

"Yes, Mrs. Banks."

Elisa and Jasmine's mom erupted in laughter. "He's been that way for a long time," Elisa said. "It will take him a while to change and get used to it."

Then their moms shared a look. What was that? Jasmine could sense the wheels turning in their heads.

"I'm guessing your arm needs to rest for a while?" her mom asked David.

Why did her mom want to know? It seemed like a simple question, but she guessed her mom was up to something.

"The doctor says I have to rest my wrist for a week," David said.

Jasmine's mom turned to her. "Did you hear that?"

Why did she have to know? How was that her business?

"He'll need your help," Jasmine's mom continued.

She knew it! Her mom was trying to push them together. No way was that going to happen. "I'll hire help for him. That should work."

"I heard you guys were working on something together," Elisa said. "You'll need to help him more than you expect."

How did she even know these things? She couldn't imagine David discussing it with his mom.

"I can't type as you can see," David said. "I'll need your help with it."

Now David had joined the fray. What was this? Gang-up time? And what was wrong with him?

"You can use your left hand and I'll get you an assistant," Jasmine said. "And you already have a secretary, remember?"

David cradled his injured arm. "I need someone who can understand all the medical lingo and make sure it makes sense," David said. "It would be too much for my secretary, and we don't have enough time before the proposal is due for multiple revisions. We'll need to meet more frequently."

Was he insane? Had he lost his mind when he got hit? Who on earth would agree to stay in constant touch with their enemy? "The remaining one week once you lose the sling will be more than enough to put the proposal together. I'll make sure my content is ready by then."

"Jasmine Banks, I thought you knew better," her mom said. "It's the least you can do considering that he saved you. Can a week be compared to the rest of your life?"

Trust Mom to deliver the low blow. It had been a mistake stepping into this cubicle. Jasmine noticed her mom glaring at her while Elisa looked at her expectantly. David was suddenly preoccupied with studying his sling.

So that's how he wanted to play it. She'd do it, but she'd make sure he regretted it. "Okay, okay. But only one week and only when I'm off work."

"I can't drive either," David said. "I'll need you to come pick me up in the morning."

Argh! She wished she could just knock him out so he would stop talking. Jasmine scowled at him instead. "Take a car service."

"But I won't be able to carry my work files to the car. Do you know how hard it is to use your left hand when you are right-handed?"

"She'll do it," Jasmine's mom said.

"Mom!" This was ridiculous. It was like a play involving her life was being acted out in front of her.

"Thank you so much!" Elisa said as she grabbed both of Jasmine's hands. "Thank you. I'll text you the address."

"So she'll be there early in the morning and after work," her mom reassured Elisa and David.

She turned to Jasmine. "It's only one week. You'll survive."

CHAPTER 16

David watched as his mom left with Mrs. Banks. Jasmine had gone with them. He chuckled. She was probably livid with him. From past experience, he knew she hated having her hands tied.

Looking back at the incident at the hotel, he'd been scared when he'd seen the car careening toward her. He'd jumped in without thinking of the danger, knowing he would never have forgiven himself if she'd gotten hurt while running away from him. It was interesting given that he'd always managed to return unscathed from any Army mission he'd been sent on, yet he'd gotten hurt just from saving Jasmine.

Was it a signal that his heart was more

involved than he thought? Was it possible she was still special to him after what she'd done and after all these years? He shook his head. Impossible! If that were the case, he wouldn't have fallen in love with Heather and planned to marry her.

But he was curious as to why she had been so angry with him at the restaurant. He'd been dwelling on it when Jasmine and her mom came in. What if what his mom said was true: that there was more to what had happened between them in the past? If that were the case, then he wanted to know what the truth was. He hadn't forgiven her for the past, but he was willing to keep an open mind till he found out the whole story. And the only way to get that, from what he could see, was to spend more time with her.

So he'd played along when their moms had been eager to get them together. The more Jasmine had resisted, the more she'd sparked a competitive spirit in him to win. And he'd succeeded.

And, no, he wasn't looking for a relationship. All he wanted was to understand what had happened years ago. If there had been a misun-derstanding between them, maybe he could gain a friend from straightening it out. And he would be killing two birds with one stone since it would also show his parents that he'd made a real effort for the arranged dates just like he'd promised. That way, they wouldn't bother him once the three weeks were up.

He smiled to himself. The next few days promised to be interesting. He had seen the look in Jasmine's eye that hinted she would get back at him.

He had a feeling he would enjoy every bit of it.

Jasmine couldn't believe she'd allowed her mom to talk her into this. She and David had both been discharged the same night from the ER, and here she was at seven a.m. the very next morning going up to his penthouse. It hadn't mattered to her mom that it was a Saturday—she'd insisted Jasmine had to be there as early as possible, even though David had no reason to head into the office for work unless he was on-call. Good thing she'd only been on regular pain killers, so she'd woken up clearheaded and had already been up for a few hours. Unfortunately, she wasn't on weekend duty, so she'd had no valid excuse to bail out of the arrangement.

She'd been amazed her mom had led the charge. Wasn't she worried about how this would affect Jasmine's reputation? Her mom had brushed away her concern, stating she was sure Jasmine could take care of herself.

But Jasmine was more worried about the gossip making its way through the hospital's grapevine. It wouldn't surprise her if some hospital employees lived in the same building given the apartment's premium downtown location. What if one of them saw her coming out of his apartment this early? They would just assume she'd slept over when she hadn't. It might not matter to others, but that wasn't who she was. She was a firm believer in sleeping in her own bed till she got married, the only exception being when she was on-call and had to stay over at the hospital.

She was fairly certain David wouldn't try anything funny. He would be in for a world of hurt if he did. She'd attended martial arts classes in the year she'd been homeschooled—she'd insisted on it after the incident in high school. Jasmine was a big advocate of women and girls being able to defend themselves against the scum of this world—the definition which applied to anyone who tried to hurt or take advantage of them as far as she was concerned.

She leaned her head against the elevator wall and took a deep breath. She wasn't sure how she felt about seeing David again. This would be the first time they'd face each other alone since the restaurant incident. Her plan right now was to get in, help him as needed, and then hightail it home. There was no need to spend more time with him than necessary. The only benefit from being here was it distracted her from dwelling on the fact that she had cancer.

It hadn't really sunk in what that meant. She'd called Dr. Allen and apologized for dropping the call and had then scheduled an appointment to see him early next week. And then she'd tossed all night thinking about it. Yet it still felt like the news belonged to someone else, not her. Did that mean she was in denial? Maybe. But how else did one deal with this life-changing news? It was easy to advise someone and another thing altogether to experience it.

The elevator reached the top floor, and the doors parted. Jasmine stepped out into a cavernous marble-tiled foyer. A glass door stood a few feet ahead and it slid open to reveal a large living room—about three times the size of her bedroom—furnished in browns and blues, Tony Landi's favorite colors from what she could remember. She looked around. Where was the fellow anyway?

"Hello, Jasmine."

Her heart rate spiked, and she turned to see David in a plain T-shirt over lounge pants, the top of his hair sporting a tousled look. It was obvious he'd just rolled out of bed, but how could bed hair be this adorable? *Stay focused, Jasmine.*

"Good morning," David said. "Why are you here so early?"

"Early? I remember a certain somebody whining about how he couldn't even get his pants on without help." Oops. Couldn't she have used a different example? She could feel her ears grow hot. And David had caught the innuendo too from the smile that crept on his face.

Then his look turned serious. "Why don't we sit?" he said and gestured to an oversized chocolate brown couch. "I think we need to clear the air about what happened on Friday night."

Well, she didn't want to talk about any of it.

"Why don't you show me what you need help with, and I'll just take care of it and get out of your way?" she said.

He stared at her for a moment, but she couldn't guess what he was thinking. Not that she cared to. "Alright," he said. "I need your help with my hair."

"Your hair?"

"I couldn't wash it last night, and it feels kind of icky especially after the accident."

Okay, she could do that. "Lead the way."

He turned and padded toward the back of the apartment till they passed a set of double doors. And that was when she realized they were in the master bedroom. An inviting majestic bed sat in the middle of the high-ceilinged room. She could just see herself curling up on the bed and taking a nap.

She drove the thought away. Definitely not happening.

David led her to a glass door and opened it. Jasmine wondered whether she'd entered a bathroom or a spa. It was expansive with a wood-themed combined shower and tub that had a rain and cascade shower head resting against a clear skylight. It sported gorgeous grey and black marble floors, a double marble vanity with copper finishings, and a large mirrored wall. It was inviting and practically calling her name.

But there was no way she was going near that bathtub. "We'll use the sink." Jasmine said quickly.

David glanced at her and said nothing. She didn't want to guess what was running through his mind. He pulled his shampoo from the shower rack and walked back to the sink. In the meantime, Jasmine had spotted the cabinet with the extra towels and had pulled two. She'd also found a small ceramic bowl she thought she could use.

She handed a towel to him. "Put this around your neck," she said.

"Don't you think it might be better if I removed my shirt so it doesn't get wet?" David asked.

"No!" Jasmine said. She could tell David was ripped from how the T-shirt fit over his muscles. There was no need to increase the temperature in the room.

"Okay," David said as he complied. "What next?"

"You'll probably have to stoop a little, but I'll need you to bend over the sink."

"Don't you think it might be easier to use the bathtub?"

There was no way she was going near that tub. She'd watched too many movies and had seen what could happen. "Let's stick with the sink, shall we?"

He bent over the first sink. "I'm ready."

Jasmine opened the hot water tap of the second sink till it was at a temperature she liked and then used the bowl to pour water over his head. She spurted some of the shampoo into her hand and rubbed it into his hair, which felt silky and smooth to touch. A coconut vanilla scent filled the air.

"This feels good," he said.

Really? Well, that wasn't what she was going for. She massaged his hair more vigorously.

"Ouch, that hurts!"

"Sorry," she said with a smile. Served him right for abandoning her.

"Are you taking your anger out on me?"

"Why would I do that?" she said sweetly. "Did you offend me?"

"Jasmine—"

"Oh, please. Just let me finish."

He kept quiet till she completed the wash. Then it was time to rinse his hair. Jasmine took water from the cold water tap and poured it over his head.

David jumped back. "Ouch! What was that for?"

Jasmine fought hard to hold back a smile. "I'm sorry. It was a mistake."

"Mistake? I'll show you what a mistake is." He pulled her to him with his left hand and held her close with his face next to hers. "Two can play this game," he whispered.

His citrusy sandalwood scent combined with the coconut vanilla aroma filled her nostrils and heightened Jasmine's senses. Her nerve endings tingled as his skin touched hers, and her heart rate began to gallop. And then he looked at her like he'd done so many years ago, like she was the only one who existed. And the butterflies in her stomach began to flutter.

He moved his face closer to hers which she'd thought would be impossible. Her breath hitched and she swallowed. Jasmine could feel his heart pounding against her chest. The butterflies in her belly went into a frenzy. She saw his eyes dart to her mouth and back to her eyes, and her defenses began to crumble. She had to get out of here.

"Let me go," she whispered.

He released his grip and stepped away so quickly that Jasmine felt a jarring effect from the loss of his arm around her.

"Never play such a dangerous game in a man's bathroom," he said in a low voice.

Jasmine stared at him, and that's when she noticed how ridiculous he looked with clumps of soap suds in his hair and soapy water running down his shirt. She erupted in laughter.

"What's so funny?" he asked.

"You look ridiculous with all that soap!"

A grin split his face. "I guess you need a look in the mirror."

Jasmine looked behind him and saw herself on the mirrored wall. She had soap all over her ponytail, neck, and blouse. "David Landi, I'll get you for this!"

"You look cute," he said, with a lazy smile.

Jasmine froze. He shouldn't be saying such things to her. He was supposed to be the enemy, the man who had hurt her. And the terrible part was she'd liked it. What was wrong with her?

The smile left her face, and she refused to meet his eye. "Let's finish up."

They completed the hair wash in uncomfortable silence.

"Thank you. Let me grab something for you to change into," David said and left the bathroom. He soon returned with a beautiful turquoise cashmere ribbed turtleneck. "You can wear this. It's new. You can change here or use the other bathroom near the living room, whichever is more comfortable for you."

Jasmine accepted it from him. "Thanks." Where had the turtleneck come from? Did it belong to a former girlfriend or fiancée? But what did it matter? It was none of her business. Nothing could happen between them. He was still Tony Landi, the man who had shattered her heart to pieces.

"I'll see you in the living room," she said and left the bathroom.

Jasmine looked up from where she sat on the couch as David walked into the living room. She'd changed into the turtleneck, which fit her to a tee. The intended owner must have been about her size. David was now dressed in a grey V-necked T-shirt over blue jeans. He walked over and sat opposite her.

She'd been here long enough. Jasmine had to keep her heart safe. For a minute she'd almost forgotten there could be nothing between them, and that was dangerous territory. It was time to leave. "Is there anything else you need me to help you with? Otherwise, I have to go," she said.

"Jasmine." Why did he say her name like that? The sound of her name on his lips brought back memories of the good times between them, reminders of a past she needed to forget. "We need to talk about what happened yesterday," he said.

Why couldn't he leave it alone? She didn't want to discuss any of it. But then she remembered what Alicia had said about keeping an open mind, so she stayed quiet.

The air between them grew awkward as Jasmine waited for him to say more.

"Jasmine," he finally said. Why did her name sound so alluring on his lips? "I had no idea you were the same person. The thought crossed my mind, but you were so passionate about fashion it seemed impossible you would leave it to become a doctor."

"Well, that's part of life." There was no way she would tell him why she'd switched her career dream. They didn't have that kind of relationship.

"I know we ended badly—"

"You mean you dumped me and hightailed it out of town."

"Hold on right there. I didn't abandon you. Have you forgotten how you broke up with me and locked me out of your life after the thing with Ken Foster?"

Jasmine straightened and her nostrils flared. "You shut me out first! I remember the look you gave me in the hallway when that monster happily told you I was a slut. You were mad at me like I had done something wrong. But guess what? That creep tried to rape me! When that didn't work, he turned around and told lies about me. It hurt so much that you believed the rumors."

David stiffened. "Rape you? I had no idea. I may have killed him if I had heard. But I wasn't angry at you. I was so mad at him for saying all that nonsense in the hallway where everyone could hear it. He ended up with some broken teeth as a result."

Jasmine's eyes widened. "You punched him?"

"I couldn't stand there and watch him ruin your reputation. But it wasn't the right thing to do, and the cops got called in. My father was able to settle the case out of court. I knew the rumors were false. There was no way you could have gone out with that weirdo. I'd heard some nasty stuff about him before. And I tried to tell you that. But you didn't pick up my calls or answer any of my texts."

"I thought you didn't want to have anything to do with me again. I waited for your call that evening, but you didn't even reach out."

David shook his head. "Not true. I was down at the police station at the time, and my parents put me on house arrest and took away my phone by the time I got home. Gabriella also got a gag order. I managed to sneak out a few times over the next few days and came by your house, but you refused to see me. And then you sent me a note through Gabriella breaking up with me. It was the straw that broke the camel's back.

I accepted the UCLA admission and never looked back."

Jasmine's insides churned. She'd been wrong. She'd lost the boy she cared for because of a misunderstanding. She'd thought he didn't care, and because it had hurt so much, she'd retreated into her shell.

She let out a long sigh, and David glanced at her. Her face grew hot at the thought he might have heard her.

"I'm glad we've cleared the air," he said.

"Me too," Jasmine responded. "So what do I call you now? David or Tony?"

"Which would you prefer?"

Tony reminded her of the past which included pieces she didn't feel like reliving. And he went by David at the hospital. "David."

"That works."

"Okay." Jasmine stood. "I need to leave now."

David got up as well. "Thanks for helping out. And you don't have to come by this evening, tomorrow, or Monday morning. I'll be spending the weekend at my parents' place."

"Good to know."

"I'll see you off."

Jasmine walked with David to the elevator. It was great to finally know the truth. Alicia had been right about keeping an open mind.

But it was water under the bridge now. Too many years had already gone by, and they were now two very different people.

And she was no longer eligible for love.

With the cancer diagnosis hanging like a knife over her head.

CHAPTER 18

David walked back into the lobby of his apartment building. He'd just seen Jasmine off. The concierge had allowed her to park out front today, but David gave her a pass that would allow her to enter the underground garage and gain access to his penthouse for her next visits.

"Excuse me, sir." David turned to the concierge. "You have a package." The young man in a crisp suit handed a long box to him.

David took the box and looked it over. The return address was a flower shop. Who could be sending him flowers? It was such a strange gift for a guy.

He thanked the concierge and took his

private elevator to his apartment. He placed the package on the kitchen countertop and used a knife to cut through the tape. He opened it to see a bouquet of wilted purple petunias and black roses. David didn't understand what petunias signified, but why would anyone send him black roses when they meant death? And wilted ones for that matter? He looked through the package for a note, but there was none.

David didn't consider himself anyone's target, but his wealth could attract all sorts of psychos out of the woodwork. So he'd always had a security firm he could call on when he needed help. The flowers could mean nothing, but he wasn't taking any chances. He picked up his phone and speed-dialed a number.

"Hello, David."

"Hi, Jack." Jack was his father's friend who had been in the Marines and then set up his own security firm when he'd retired. His company, SecureFi, provided security management to Landisil Silicone facilities and its executives around the world.

"It's been a long time. I heard you left the Army."

"It was time."

"I hear you. What can I do for you today?"

"I just received a strange package delivered to my apartment. It contained wilted petunias and black roses, but had no note."

"That's ominous. I'll send someone to pick it up. I'll let you know what I find out within the next twenty-four hours. But it might be a good idea for you to have a security detail."

"Let's hold off on that for now. I'll let you know if I need it. I can still protect myself, you know."

"Yes, in normal circumstances, but you have a sprained wrist."

"How did you know that? Have you been keeping tabs on me?"

Jack laughed. "Your father told me. You know we go fishing together most Saturdays."

Right. The last thing he needed was someone following him around. He'd had enough of that living-on-the-edge stuff while in the Army.

"Okay, let me know once you find something," David said.

"Will do." The line went dead.

Within a few minutes, the concierge informed him that a Mr. Gray was waiting for a package. David sent the elevator down with it.

Jack definitely had someone following him—there was no way Mr. Gray could have arrived that fast. David's father must have put him up to it. He resolved to tell his father later in the evening to call them off. He hated being followed, and he was sure Jasmine would detest it as well, which is what would happen once they realized she was visiting his apartment.

Jasmine. He'd been surprised to see her here so early. He'd thought she'd blow him off and not come.

She'd looked nice in the turtleneck. He'd bought it on a whim as a surprise gift for Gabriella. It had turned out to be the wrong size for her. He'd planned to return it but never got the chance. David had found it in a shopping bag in his closet as he'd unpacked his things. Thank goodness he'd kept it; Jasmine might not have been comfortable wearing one of his shirts. Which he wouldn't have minded, if he was truthful to himself.

He'd also enjoyed seeing a bit of the old playful Jasmine as she'd washed his hair. It had taken him back to their old memories.

He hadn't known that Ken Foster had tried to rape her. He couldn't imagine how she must have felt being attacked by him when she'd been the victim. It was a good thing he hadn't heard about it—God probably knew he might have harmed Ken Foster for it. He'd been young and foolish then but had always felt a fierce protectiveness toward Jasmine. That was why her rejection at that time had hurt. Now the truth was out, and it was freeing to know.

But that didn't mean they could start off where they'd stopped. They had both grown and changed.

And he wasn't interested in a relationship, despite how much brightness she brought to his life or the way the touch of her hand ignited his skin.

CHAPTER 19

The weekend had been a blur of swirling feelings about the cancer. Being the only one to know and not sharing it with anyone had not been as easy as Jasmine had envisioned. She'd picked up her phone a couple of times to call her mom, but she had stopped each time. It was enough that she alone bore the pain. She could not allow her mom to experience the same.

She'd seen firsthand how devastated her mom could be when she'd told her about the almost rape. Her mom had blamed herself for not protecting Jasmine, and the trip abroad had been as much a healing time for her mom as for her. Jasmine couldn't go through that again.

She'd been tempted to tell Alicia and Dana, but they'd both been on-call that weekend. Jasmine had also been afraid the news would ruin their wedding planning. So the weekend had been a time of restlessness, tossing, and turning. Only when she'd prayed had she been able to get some sleep.

And that was one area she'd been slacking off on. She'd been so consumed by her fears and worry that she'd forgotten to talk to God, the one person she needed most to get through this. So she'd remedied that. The problem didn't go away, but she'd started the new week with a lot more peace than she'd thought possible.

She'd also not heard from David the rest of the weekend. Not that she had expected to. But she'd remembered how they used to talk about everything together in the past, and so she'd wished for a little bit of that. But wishes were not horses, so that hadn't happened.

Monday had arrived as busy as usual. Between prepping and completing her OR cases and seeing to consults from the ER and other departments, the day had gone by quickly, and it had been time to sign off before she'd known it.

Jasmine was now on her way up to David's penthouse. She'd texted him to confirm he was at home before heading out. Friday couldn't come too soon as far as she was concerned. And then she wouldn't be required to come here anymore.

The elevator doors slid open, and she stepped through the foyer into the living room.

"Jasmine!" The petite black-haired knockout that was Gabriella Landi stood in front of her with a big smile on her face. "David, you didn't tell me Jasmine was coming over," she called over her shoulder.

It was great to see Gabriella, and Jasmine gave her a hug. "It's not what you think." At Gabriella's raised brow, "My mom and yours put me up to this."

"Hold on. So the arranged date thingy is real? I thought my parents were pulling my leg when they mentioned it. Hmmm. No wonder David has been smiling more."

"I don't know what you are talking about," David said as he came into view looking delicious enough to eat in his blue polo shirt and tan shorts. He still had his right arm in a sling. "Hello, Jasmine." He gave her a smile, and that adorable dimple appeared.

Her skin began to tingle. What was it about this man that he had such an effect on her? She wasn't sure how long she could take it before her defenses came crashing down, and it seemed David had help already, which was great because she was exhausted. She had to get away ASAP. "Hi, David. I'll just leave since Gabriella is here. You probably don't need my help."

"Oh, please." Gabriella grabbed Jasmine's arm and led her further into the living room. "If you leave, I'll go also. And I'll tell my mom that you abandoned him."

"Stop threatening her, Ella," David said.

"See what I mean? He is already defending you over his own sister."

"Jasmine, we do need your help," David said. "We've been brainstorming ideas on how to launch the Landisil-IntimiRose brand." Seeing the look on Jasmine's face, he said, "Don't worry. I'm sure our parents will still make the deal work without us being in a relationship."

"You mean *you* have been brainstorming," Gabriella said. "Jasmine, I came here just to check on him and he strong-armed me into talking about the deal. He seems to be going stir-crazy with all the time on his hands."

Jasmine gave him a questioning look. Wasn't he supposed to have been at the office?

David shrugged. "It's not my fault. The department gave me the week off till the sling goes away. They don't want anything to affect the healing of my wrist given how important it is for me as a surgeon."

"I'm sorry," Jasmine said.

"Don't be," David replied. "I'd gladly do it again."

"Wow!" Gabriella said. "David and Jasmine, I'm loving you two right now."

"Shut up!" David and Jasmine said in unison.

"See? You guys are even in sync."

Jasmine shook her head. She'd forgotten how annoying Gabriella could be sometimes.

"Come on, let me show you something," Gabriella said as she dragged Jasmine toward the dining area where a massive custom table and bench set stood.

Jasmine peered closer. Was that a bra mixed up with all the papers strewn on top of the table?

"Yes, that's an Intimi-Rose bra. We wanted to study its design in detail," Gabriella said.

Jasmine gave David a bemused look.

"Hey, I had nothing to do with it. It was all Gabriella," David said in his defense.

"David, it's only a bra," Gabriella said. "It's not dangerous. And I'm surprised at your reaction, given how much you work with women's breasts." Gabriella picked up the bra and flung it at David, who dodged. The bra landed on the couch, but scattered some papers that had been piled in a heap.

"Ella!"

Gabriella grinned. "You have to own it. Touching a bra is no big deal."

Jasmine smiled at their exchange. It seemed some things never changed.

David tried to gather up the papers that had fallen from the couch, but he made more mess instead. Jasmine bent and helped him till all the sheets were back together.

"Thanks," David said.

"My pleasure," Jasmine responded. "I have to go though. Gabriella is here, so you don't really need me. And it has been a long day."

Gabriella pouted. "Do you have to?"

Jasmine nodded. She turned back to David. "Are we still meeting tomorrow at the hospital?"

"Yes, I'll just come in for that and then leave."

"Sounds good."

"Let me walk you down."

"You don't have to. I'll be fine."

"Really, I insist."

"Okay."

"I'll be back," he said to Gabriella.

Gabriella gave Jasmine another hug. "Good to see you. Don't be a stranger."

"I won't."

Soon David and Jasmine were in the elevator as it sped to the underground parking garage. The doors pinged open, and they stepped out.

"Dr. Banks!" a voice called out.

Who could be calling her? Jasmine turned to see Nurse Munroe, a buxom middle-aged surgical nurse known for her sharp tongue, marching toward them. This was her worst luck ever.

"I knew it was you!" Nurse Munroe said triumphantly. "What are you doing here?"

"Good evening, Nurse Munroe." Jasmine

said. Good thing she probably didn't know David or it would be a disaster.

Nurse Munroe peered closer at David. "Wait! It's Dr. Landi, right? The new surgeon?" She looked from Jasmine to David. "What are you two doing here?"

Jasmine froze.

Her worst fears had just come true.

CHAPTER 20

*D*avid had seen Jasmine stiffen, and he understood immediately. Nurse Munroe had to be an active member of the hospital's rumor mill.

He stepped forward. "Nurse Munroe, it's great to meet you. I didn't know you lived in this building."

"I do! What about you?" Then she seemed to notice his arm. "What happened?"

"Just a little accident. I can't do much with it though. Dr. Banks was kind enough to help me out a few minutes ago." He turned to Jasmine. "Thanks for your assistance, Dr. Banks. Please tell Prof. Morgan I'll call her soon."

Jasmine nodded. "Have a good evening," she said to Nurse Munroe and walked off toward her car.

David turned back to Nurse Munroe and flashed her a brilliant smile. "It was nice meeting you. I hope you have a good day too."

He turned and headed for the elevator bank. Hopefully, that was enough to mitigate any damage Nurse Munroe's tongue could do.

David stepped out of the elevator and headed to the concierge's desk. Another young man, different from the one he'd seen previously, manned the desk.

"Good evening, Dr. Landi," the young man said, his bulbous nose tweaking in accompaniment. His tag had the name James on it.

"Hello, James," David said.

"A Miss Hamilton stopped by and dropped this," James said as he extended a long package to him. Miss Hamilton was David's secretary. "She said you might need it urgently."

The package looked so similar to the first one

he'd received, David motioned for James to drop the package on the reception desk. Then he pulled out his phone and speed-dialed Jack. Jack picked up on the first ring.

"We have another one," David said. "It was sent to my office instead." Jack and his team hadn't found any information from the first box, and the flower shop address had been fake. Even the packaging could have been bought in any local store. David hoped they would get something this time around.

"Have you opened it?"

"No. I figured you might want to check for fingerprints."

"We didn't find any on the last one either. This person is careful. There may not be prints on this one too. Why don't you open it?"

"Okay." David requested for a box cutter from the concierge who handed him one. He sliced the tape and opened up a flap. "Same wilted petunias and black roses, but the ratios seem different."

"How so?"

"The bouquet looks bigger and now there are more roses than petunias. Oh, and there is what looks like blood on the roses, though

I'm not certain if it's of animal or human origin."

"I think this person is escalating. His or her rage and anger toward you is increasing, but it seems there is a greater desire to see you dead. This person knows you. He or she knows where you live and work."

Who could it be? He couldn't remember harming anyone intentionally.

"David, I think it's time we put a security detail on you," Jack insisted.

"No, I don't think it's gotten to that point yet, and we don't know what this person would do if they find out I have one."

"I don't think—"

"It's what I want."

"Okay, we'll hold off for now. I'll send someone to pick up the package. Just leave it with the concierge."

"I will. Thanks, Jack." David ended the call.

He hadn't told Jack, but he planned to use himself as bait. That was why he had refused the security detail. That way, the person would just assume he could reach David, instead of looking for alternate ways to harm him, which could mean hurting someone around him like Jasmine or Gabriella. He also had a feeling an attack would happen soon, though there was no concrete evidence to suggest so.

There wasn't anything else he could do for now.

He would wait for the perp's next move.

And he would be ready.

Jasmine wrung her hands as she sat opposite Dr. Allen, a long-limbed surgeon with wide black brows and a head full of hair, and waited for him to speak. She'd arrived early for her Tuesday afternoon appointment in the hope that she would finish on time to rejoin her team for clinic hours. Dr. Allen had been gracious enough to accommodate her at such short notice.

She'd already met David earlier in the day, and they had talked through the draft of the proposal document they had pulled together. Jasmine had updated the changes live as they discussed and had sent him the revised document once they'd finished. David was going to make any final changes before sharing it with Prof. Morgan to review. There had been no time to chat or grab lunch since Jasmine had to rush over for her appointment.

She'd also been relieved there had been no rumors about David and her at the hospital. David's charm must have worked on Nurse Munroe.

"So have you decided what treatment option you would prefer?" Dr. Allen asked. They'd discussed the pathology results, and Dr. Allen had laid out which treatment alternatives would work best in her case as well as the risks associated with each one.

Jasmine took a deep breath and exhaled. She'd already made up her mind before coming, but she'd waited to hear him out in case she'd missed anything. But it still wasn't easy saying it out loud. "A double mastectomy followed by chemotherapy."

"Are you sure?"

"Yes, but I'd like to have the breast reconstruction in the same surgery."

"That would mean a much longer OR time, but that should be fine given your health risk profile. Let me see what dates I have available."

Dr. Allen pulled up his calendar on the computer that sat on the L-section of his desk. "How about Thursday of next week? The next available date after that would be in two months."

That soon? She needed more time to mentally prepare herself. But two months was too long to wait. She had no idea what the cancer would do by then. She could do this. "Next week would work."

"Okay. I've added you to my schedule. We'll also have a medical oncologist, Dr. Korode, as part of the team. She would be in charge of your chemotherapy regimen. Please see my office manager on your way out. She'll talk you through the next steps and will also reach out to you over the next couple of days to make sure everything is set for the surgery."

"Sounds good."

"Do you have any more questions for me?"

"Not at this time."

"Feel free to reach out if any arise, alright? We are here for you."

Jasmine stood. "Thanks. I will," she said before leaving his office.

Jasmine left the breast clinic and walked down the hallway to the elevator. It was still surreal that she was going to have her breasts removed in a few days. She had made her peace when she decided that was the best option for her, but now she felt some trepidation at the thought of losing both breasts so soon.

They'd been a favorite part of her for so long that it was hard to imagine them gone. True, she was having reconstruction done, but they would never be the same again. What if her appearance changed? And she would always know what she had was fake.

And there were complications with implants to consider. What if the scar tissue forced them to harden? Then she would have rocks as breasts and would need another surgery just to release the scar tissue. She might also have to deal with phantom pain and loss of breast sensation.

And if by some miraculous chance, she entered into a relationship and got married, how would she feel about expressing love physically with her spouse? Would she ever feel comfortable enough to allow him to touch her, knowing she had implants and not real breasts, and would he accept her, fake breasts and all? It was one thing for him to say so before the marriage and another to actually embrace it after.

Jasmine shook her head. What was she thinking? She'd forgotten the most important reason for the double mastectomy: she would be cancer-free. She would live. And chances of a reoccurrence would be greatly reduced since all the breast tissue would be gone. The fear that the cancer would come back wouldn't be hanging around her neck, waiting to choke her. That alone made the double mastectomy worth it.

Her only regret was she couldn't tell her family and friends. The emotional support would have made all the difference. Well, she had God, and He was more than enough. *Thank you, God, for being there.*

She could get through this. All she had to do was keep busy till the date of the surgery.

She pressed the elevator button that led to the ObGyn floor where her clinic patients were waiting.

CHAPTER 22

*D*avid flexed his wrist. It felt good to be out of the sling and regain use of his right hand. But it also meant Jasmine would no longer come to his home to help him. He'd enjoyed her brief visits, though she'd always left as soon as she could.

She had brought a brightness to his home that he hadn't thought possible. He would miss it, but the memories would remain and for that he was grateful. She would take off for sure if she saw his sling-less arm today, and he wanted to have dinner with her before she did, both to thank her and to get to know her more. The Tuesday lunch would have worked as well, but that had been cancelled.

His doctor, a white-haired orthopedic surgeon, smiled at him. "You are now cleared for a return to full duty. I'll send the information to HR."

"Thanks. Can I keep the sling?"

"Sure. But what do you need it for?"

David smiled. He would put the sling back on before Jasmine arrived and surprise her by taking it off after dinner. She would be very happy.

Yes, that would work.

He couldn't wait to see her face when he did.

CHAPTER 23

*J*asmine couldn't believe her eyes at the spread on David's dining table. There were bowls of roasted tomato soup served with crackers, chicken parmesan with linguine and broccoli, zucchini stuffed with sausage and breadcrumbs, and toasted mini bread slices topped with a dollop of milky cheese and strawberries and lightly sprinkled with what looked like a blend of balsamic vinegar and honey. Was there a party supposed to take place here she wasn't aware of?

"Please, sit," David said.

"What's going on?" she asked, as she sat on the bench.

"I just wanted to say thank you for helping

me. The sling is coming off soon, and we were able to finish the proposal much earlier than we'd planned." David's hiatus from work had given them extra time to put the document together. David had ended up dictating his notes which his secretary had transcribed. It was now in the hands of Prof. Morgan, who'd said she would get back to them in a few days.

"I'm not sure I did much in helping you, and I just took care of the sections I was supposed to in the proposal."

"But your being here while I worked on the document made a difference. Why don't we eat?"

The meal was delicious. Jasmine couldn't remember when she'd been this stuffed. "This was really good," she said as they cleared the dishes and carried them to the sink. Jasmine chose to wash while David opted to rinse and dry them.

"Thank you. I enjoyed making it," he said.

Jasmine's eyes widened. "You cook?" There was nothing as sexy as a man who could cook. "How did you?"

"A secret. I learned how to cook in college.

Eating pizza all the time got old pretty fast. Did you go to college in Dexington?"

"No, college in Boston and then back to Dexington for medical school. I'm assuming UCLA all the way?"

"Yep."

"Do you miss the West Coast?"

"Sometimes, but Dexington has its charm too, and my family is here."

"So I have to ask. Why the Army? You never struck me as the military type." Jasmine noted a look of pain cross David's features and then disappear.

"I needed a change," he said. "It was the best option available at the time."

Jasmine knew better than to dig further. He'd tell her if he wanted to.

"So why did you become a doctor?" he asked. "I'd always thought I'd see your designs coming down the runway."

She wasn't ready to share why. "Life happened, and being an ObGyn became a passion of mine."

Jasmine could tell he wanted to know more, but he didn't press her. By now all the dishes had been set up to dry in the dish drying cabinet. "Do you want coffee?" he asked instead.

"Yes. But let me make it as a thank you for the wonderful meal."

"Sounds good." His phone rang. "Give me one second." He stepped away into the living room to take the call.

Jasmine pulled two mugs from the cup rack and examined them. One was a purple iridescent cup with mini stars in white all around it, while the other had a blue and brown striped design. They were very different, yet so beautiful. As she placed them on the kitchen countertop, the purple one slipped and crashed on the floor.

Jasmine jumped back as the sound echoed in the room and the ceramic shattered into a million pieces.

"Are you alright?" She looked up to see David had returned to the kitchen. He stared and now was staring at her with concern.

"I'm fine."

He bent down. "Let me ... " His eyes widened. "No, it can't be."

"What is it?"

"How could you?" The angry sparks from his eyes could have scorched her.

"What did I do?"

"Not this ..." He reached out to touch the broken pieces.

She grabbed his arm. "Don't touch—"

He flung her hand away. "Leave me alone!"

Jasmine stepped back. The cup must have been special for David to be reacting this way. "I'm sorry. I didn't—"

"Please leave," he said through gritted teeth. He began to pick up the pieces one by one.

Jasmine turned and ran into the living room. She picked up her bag and raced to the entrance, jabbing the elevator button multiple times. David had every right to be angry, but he shouldn't have spoken to her that way. It had only been a mistake. She'd thought at least they could remain friends, but that was out of the window now. Not with the way he'd just treated her.

She wiped the tears from her eyes as she took the elevator down to the parking lot. There was no way she was coming back here, even if he still needed her help. And the proposal was done so that couldn't be used as an excuse. She would tell her parents the arranged-marriage date was over. They had promised they wouldn't impose their will on her. She was done with David.

The elevator reached the garage, and she stepped out.

Strong arms grabbed her from behind.

CHAPTER 24

David was mad at himself for his outburst. Jasmine didn't deserve it. It was clearly a mistake, and there was no way she could have known that the mug had been a present from Heather. He'd hurt her, and there was a strong chance he would lose her if he didn't make things right immediately. That would be devastating, and it meant only one thing: he liked Jasmine a lot, more than he imagined.

He jumped up from the kitchen floor and raced out of the apartment. On the way down, he prayed she was still in the garage.

The elevator stopped at the parking level, and David rushed out. That was when he heard the muffled noise.

His head jerked in the direction of the sound, and he saw a man dressed in black dragging a woman with a swinging red ponytail by the neck and heading toward a far corner of the garage where a red pickup truck was parked.

David's blood ran cold. Jasmine! He didn't know who the man was, but he had to save her no matter what it took.

He sprinted after the man as fast as he could. The sling was holding him back, so David flung it away. The man must have realized someone was following him, because he looked back. David saw the face and gasped. It was Simon Carter, a man he had saved back in Germany!

What was he doing here, and why was he kidnapping Jasmine? David had saved Simon's life after he'd stepped on an IED a few weeks before Simon was supposed to return stateside after completing his second tour of duty. He'd then operated on him for some of the reconstructive surgery Simon had needed for his severely burned face.

Then David remembered Simon had mentioned that his mom owned a flower shop. Could it be …Was this related to the flowers he'd been receiving? That meant David was the target! So, Simon had taken Jasmine to punish David. No! He couldn't let Jasmine suffer for whatever it was Simon thought David had done.

David reached Simon, but what he saw next stunned him. It seemed the momentary distraction from David had been all Jasmine needed. One minute Simon was gripping her, the next he was on the floor with his lights out. Jasmine stood next to him coughing and breathing deeply.

David grabbed her in a bear hug. "Are you okay? I'm so sorry. It's all my fault."

"You're suffocating me!" she said, pushing against him.

"Oh, sorry." He released her. "Are you hurt?"

"Could you call 9-1-1 first?"

CHAPTER 25

"Are you sure you're okay?" David asked Jasmine.

She struggled to hold back a chuckle. This was the fifth time he'd asked. She'd never seen him so worried. He kept checking her to make sure she wasn't hurt. And she liked how it made her feel, like she was important to him.

She'd been caught unawares when the wiry man grabbed her. But as he'd dragged her along, she'd remembered the attack by Ken Foster. She'd sworn after that incident she'd never be a victim again, so she'd forced herself to maintain her composure like her martial arts instructor had taught her and waited for an opportunity.

The distraction from David had provided

one. She'd kicked the man with a force fueled by anger at all the monsters who preyed on innocent women and who thought she was fair play, knocking him out. And surprisingly, she'd felt calm after the experience instead of going into shock. It was like it had been the confirmation and validation she'd needed that she wasn't weak. That she was strong enough to take care of herself. But it was also nice that David was here too.

But who was the guy? She peered closely at him where he lay passed out. She hadn't seen his face before. But David had said something about it being his fault.

"Do you know him?" she asked David.

"Yes."

"You do?"

"He's someone I saved from the brink of death in the Army."

So, David had been the target. Still, that didn't make any sense. "But why would he come after you if you saved him? And me?"

David told her about the flowers. "Maybe he thought we were a couple and he could get to me through you, though I don't understand why he would hate me in the first place."

"Maybe he resents you."

"Why would he?"

"He could have had a hard time adjusting back home and wished he had died instead. He may have blamed you for not letting him die."

"Possibly. Maybe he'll tell the police the truth when he regains consciousness."

The cops arrived at that moment and escorted the guy into custody. They took Jasmine's and David's statements, and promised to reach out if they had any other questions.

The paramedics checked Jasmine out, but she declined to go to the hospital. There was no need for it since she wasn't hurt. David also stepped away to make a call—it seemed he was updating someone on what had happened, from the bits of conversation she overheard.

"I'm glad that is over," David said as he rejoined her. "Would you like to go upstairs?"

"No, I'd prefer to go home." That was when she noticed the sling was gone. "What happened to the sling? Is your arm okay?"

"It's fine. The surgeon gave me the okay to remove it today."

So he had deceived her. She had to know the

reason for it. "So why were you still wearing it earlier?"

"I was afraid you would leave and not stay for dinner if you found out. I had planned to tell you later, but the incident with the mug happened. Which brings me to my original reason for coming after you: I'm sorry, Jasmine. I'm sorry for getting mad at you about the mug."

"Why did you?"

"It was a special gift from someone. But that wasn't enough reason to blow up on you."

Now she felt bad. She'd destroyed something that was important to him. "I'm sorry for breaking the mug."

"It's okay. I'm glad I came after you, though you clearly handled things yourself. I was scared at the thought of losing you. That's when I realized one thing." David moved closer and held her by the shoulders. "I like you, Jasmine Banks. A lot. And I want to keep seeing you. Would you go out on a date with me?"

A warm tingle filled Jasmine's body. Wow, that came out of left field. Sure, she'd felt the chemistry between them, but he hadn't shown any sign he was interested. And she loved the idea of going out with him.

But that was all it could be. The cancer had pretty much sealed her fate and eliminated any chance of a relationship with David Landi even if she wanted to. "There's something I have to tell you first," she said.

"Are you in love with someone else?" he asked in a worried tone.

"No."

"Are you a criminal?"

She chuckled at that one. "No."

He smiled. "Then nothing else matters. Is it a yes?"

He looked at her with a gaze so full of hope that she didn't have the heart to tell him no. And a part of her wanted to go out with him, even if it was just for a little while before she had the surgery. Who knew if she would ever have the chance again? But it could also break her heart when the time came to part ways.

"I mean it, Jasmine. Nothing else matters."

She took a deep breath. Maybe it was worth the risk. "Yes."

CHAPTER 26

Jasmine examined her profile in the full-length mirror. She looked good, if she said so herself. She'd gone for a softer look than she typically wore—a floral long-sleeved dress in red, gold, and green that hugged her figure in the right places, paired with gold strappy shoes and simple gold earrings. She'd let down her hair for a change, and it flowed down her back in soft waves. A dark green snakeskin belt completed the look and accentuated the green in her eyes.

Earlier in the day, she'd gotten a call from the police about the attacker. He'd regained consciousness and had sung like a bird. And she'd been right. He'd confessed he resented

David for saving his life. His mom had rejected him, calling him a freak because of his damaged face. His neighbors had avoided him and warned their kids to stay away. Even the girl he'd been engaged to had taken one look at his face and married her co-worker instead. And he'd found it hard to find a decent job. He'd wished he had died instead and had blamed David for everything.

So, he'd tracked down David's location. He'd then followed him home from work. He'd watched David see Jasmine off a few times and had assumed she was his girlfriend. Since his woman had left him, he'd figured David didn't deserve one either. So he'd targeted Jasmine instead.

The police informed her he'd been charged but was also undergoing psychiatric evaluation. The Army had also gotten involved in the case. Jasmine was just glad it was over and wanted to put everything behind her.

"Wow, you look stunning!" Jasmine turned to see Dana standing in the room with Jasmine's door ajar. She hadn't even heard the door open. "I've never seen you dressed like this. And your hair!"

"Thank you." A pain jabbed in her heart as she touched her hair, at the thought that she might never have it this way again once she started chemotherapy. But it could always grow back.

Dana stepped forward and sat on her bed. "I'm assuming you are going out with Mr. Arranged-Marriage Date. It's Friday night after all."

"His name is David Landi."

"Now where have I heard that name before? Wait! You mean David Landi, the new cutie at the hospital? I thought your date was with Tony Landi. Jasmine, you've been hiding stuff!"

If only Dana knew what else she hadn't told her—the cancer for one. "Tony Landi turned out to be David Landi," Jasmine said. "And there really was a misunderstanding about what happened between us."

"Are you serious? I thought stuff like that only happened in the movies. I'm guessing you are liking Mr. Landi, eh?"

"Well, I agree he's cute."

"You don't say." Dana got up and peered at Jasmine's face. "I think it's more than that. You like him a lot."

"I do not!"

"Then tell me why your ears are turning red." Jasmine grabbed a pillow and smacked Dana. "Hey, what was that for?"

"You need to shut up."

"For that, I'm going to call Alicia and tell her you've fallen in love with Mr. Hottie." Dana pulled her phone from her pocket and pressed a speed-dial number. "Hey, Alicia—"

Jasmine grabbed the phone. "Don't you even think about it!" She ended the call.

Dana grinned. "You know she's going to call back."

Jasmine flopped on her bed. "You are so evil." She turned to Dana. "I'm not sure how I feel about him. I like him, but I don't know."

"What are you afraid of?"

Jasmine gave her a sharp look. "What do you mean?"

"I've seen you turn down guys over the years and do it with confidence. This is the first time a guy is getting to you, and I think it's because you like him. So you have to be afraid of something to be hesitating."

Dana was right. Jasmine was afraid that David might leave her if he found out about the cancer. She wouldn't blame him, but her heart would be ripped to pieces. She wasn't sure she wanted to take that chance. But she couldn't tell Dana what the reason was.

"I'll think about it. But right now, I have a date to get to," Jasmine said.

Her phone chimed. She picked it up from the bedside table and checked the screen. It was a text message from David. He was outside. "I have to go. Mr. Hottie has arrived. Why don't you come and say hello?"

"Some other time. When you are no longer of two minds. Make sure you have fun, okay?"

"Yes, ma'am."

"Now go before the Cinderella carriage turns into a pumpkin!"

CHAPTER 27

*J*asmine laughed as she stared at the Ford F-150 Limited truck parked on the curb. "You haven't changed."

David opened the passenger door for her. "I love my trucks. Comfortable yet perfect for towing sporting equipment when needed. But they don't hold a candle to how beautiful you look tonight." And he meant it. She looked sensational in her outfit, and he had no words for her hair. It was glorious, and all he wanted to do was run his hands through it.

Jasmine blushed. He loved the way it went perfectly with her red hair.

"Why, thank you, Dr. Landi," Jasmine said as she stepped into the truck. "You don't look bad yourself." David was dressed in a white button-down oxford shirt paired with khaki chinos and matching boat shoes. A dark blue blazer sporting a polka dot pocket square completed the ensemble.

David closed the door after her and then walked around to the driver's side and slid in. He started the truck and drove into the street. "I assume you got the call from the police," he said.

"Yes, they told me why the man targeted me."

"I'm sorry it happened."

"Don't be. It's over, and I'm fine. So where are we going?"

It was obvious she didn't want to talk about it anymore. She seemed calm, and he decided it was best to let it be. "We are headed to my favorite restaurant. I like to go there whenever I'm in town."

"Don't tell me it's the chicken and noodle place we used to go to in high school. I'm way too overdressed for that."

"Is that place still there? I heard rumors they closed shop after the owner died."

"It's still open, but the taste is not the same."

"So many memories in that hole-in-the-wall," David said.

"I used to wonder why you loved that place so much. Then I figured it out. The seats were tiny, so it was a good excuse for you to put your arm around my shoulders."

David chuckled. "Hey, that wasn't the reason why!"

Jasmine raised an eyebrow. "Yeah? Then how come you never sat opposite me?"

David laughed. "Because my legs were too long. There wouldn't have been enough space for you to stretch yours."

He could tell Jasmine didn't believe him. "Really?" she said.

"I'm serious. Scout's honor."

"Okay, if you say so."

He had missed this. The camaraderie and easy laughter. "Whatever happened to everyone we went to high school with?"

"Some have moved away. Others still live in town. There is an annual high school reunion. You should come."

"Maybe I will."

"On second thought, don't come."

David glanced at her. "Why?"

"I have no energy to be knocking people off you."

David erupted in laughter. "That wouldn't be so bad. Maybe it will make you appreciate me more."

"I appreciate you just fine even in ways you can't imagine."

"Like?"

"I doubt you want to know. Don't think I haven't noticed that you blush just as well as I do."

Was there anything she wouldn't say? She really hadn't changed. He hadn't realized how much he'd missed her until now.

"So what do you do for fun?" David asked.

"I'm a thrill hunter."

He gave her a quizzical look. "A what?"

"I love to try out anything sporty that would get my adrenaline going."

David gave her an incredulous look. "Are you serious? You? Weren't you the one afraid of heights?"

"I still am a little, but I've learned to try new things."

"Like?"

"I skydive, scuba dive, hang glide, mountain climb, and run the triathlon when I can."

Who was this Jasmine and what had they done with the one he used to know? "I love scuba diving."

"You were always fascinated with water."

"Maybe we could go together sometime. Which mountains have you climbed?"

"Mount Kilimanjaro, Denali, and Annapurna. I haven't gone recently though. Maybe I'll celebrate with a climb when I finish residency."

"You're in your third year, right?"

"Yep. And you're an attending. It feels weird knowing you are like my boss."

"Thank goodness I'm not your boss. If not, we wouldn't be able to go out like this." David slowed to a stop. "We are here."

CHAPTER 28

"I wouldn't have guessed you loved Japanese food," Jasmine said as a waitress dressed in a kimono led them to the private terrace. "I've never eaten in a traditional Japanese restaurant before."

"So you are a traditional Japanese food virgin."

Jasmine laughed. "If you say so."

"You'll like it here."

The waitress stopped as they arrived in front of a door made of translucent paper bonded over a lattice of bamboo and wood. She slid it open and waved them in before closing the door behind them.

Jasmine looked around. Lush colorful flowers—in contrast against the room's subdued bamboo floors—filled the space behind the enclosed glass walls, giving off a greenhouse vibe. "I didn't expect this."

"This is the owner's take on adding a modern twist to traditional." David removed his shoes by the door and Jasmine did the same.

"So are we sitting cross-legged?" Jasmine asked as she looked at the low traditional table with cushions on the floor. "I'm not sure how my dress works for that."

"Don't worry." David pressed a hidden panel on the wall beside him, and the floorboard under the table slid out of view to reveal a sunken floor.

"That's interesting."

"It's more efficient and leaves it up to the customer to decide how they want to sit."

Jasmine sat on one of the cushions and dropped her legs into the sunken space. David did the same. "Ooh, it's heated," she said. "And there is enough space to play footsie," she muttered to herself.

Her face heated as she realized she'd said it

out loud. What was it about David that loosened her tongue? She might need to put a lock on her mouth soon if she wasn't careful.

David gave her a knowing smile that told her he'd heard her.

"I'm not saying I want to do that," she clarified.

Time to change the subject before the conversation went off the rails. "So how do we order?"

"We are having *omakase,* where the chef recommends our order," David said. "You don't have any food allergies, right?"

"None at all."

"Good. The food will be here shortly."

As if on cue, the door slid open and the waitress reentered with a cart. She placed the dishes on the table and left.

"Let's see what we have here," David said.

Instead of the typical American menu—appetizer, main course, and dessert—all the dishes were served at the same time. There were plates of steamed rice mixed with seasoned seaweed, miso soup topped with green onion and tofu, pickled vegetables—ginger, cucumber, and eggplant—and lotus, a hot pot vegetable-protein dish called oden, and sweet rice cakes.

Jasmine wiped her hands with the steamy hand towel the waitress had brought before blessing the food and diving in.

The meal was delicious. With each dish, she felt her palate awaken more and more till the flavors were exploding in her mouth. David and Jasmine laughed and talked about their past between bites of food.

She leaned back when she couldn't eat another morsel. "This was great. I enjoyed it," she said. "I can see myself coming back here another day."

"I'm glad you liked it," David responded.

"But there's one thing missing that would have completed the meal."

"What's that?" David asked.

"Music. The kind that you used to play for me—simple but heartwarming. I loved it. It always touched my heart. Do you still play?"

David leaned back. "Occasionally, till a few years ago. And now life is just too busy. Maybe one day."

The waitress returned, cleared the table, and served them Japanese green tea, which was a satisfying ending to a fantastic meal.

It had been a wonderful date so far with

good food and great company. But did she deserve this? Wasn't she setting him up for disappointment since she hadn't told him about the cancer? Yes, talking about cancer wasn't what one did on a normal first date, but this was different since they'd known each other before. An omission such as this could well be considered deceit if she planned to see him again.

And Jasmine wanted to. The more time she spent with him, the more she wanted to keep doing so. And there was nothing as good as starting a relationship on a clean slate. Which meant she had to tell him, especially since she was going to have the surgery soon. There was no way he wouldn't find out about it since he worked in the same hospital. It was better he heard it directly from her than from someone else.

"David, I have something I need to tell you."

His pager pinged. "One second," he said. David pulled out his pager and checked the screen. Then he looked up at Jasmine. "I'm sorry, I have to go back to the hospital. There is an emergency surgery I need to take care of. What was it you wanted to tell me?"

There was no way she could mention it now.

It would distract him during the surgery and there would be a person's life on the line. She would have to tell him another time. She flashed him a small smile. "It can wait. Go."

"I'll drop you off. It's the least I can do."

CHAPTER 29

"BP has crashed!" a nurse called out. "I can't feel her pulse!"

David's heart raced as he looked at Heather's heart rhythm on the monitor screen. It had flatlined. A blare from the monitor pierced the air. David paced at her bedside. *Please, Heather, don't leave me.*

"Paddles ready?" her doctor asked. "One hundred joules."

"Everybody step back!" another nurse called. The paddles discharged, and Heather jerked.

David's eyes flashed back to the monitor. No change. His heart rate galloped, and he wrung his hands.

"One milligram of epinephrine IV, then

another one hundred joules," her doctor called out.

Her body sprang up from the bed at the second discharge from the paddles. Only a continuous beep from the monitor filled the room. The nurse shook her head at the doctor.

The doctor closed her eyelids. "Time of death is—"

"Nooo!" David screamed.

His eyes jerked open. His pulse raced, and his heart pounded against his rib cage. David was back in his bed, his body riddled with cold sweat, and his hair in disarray.

He sat up and waited for his heart rate to slow down. It had been a long time since he'd had a nightmare about Heather's death. He'd had them regularly in the first year after she'd passed away, but it had been almost nine months since he'd had the last one. It must have been triggered by the patient they'd almost lost tonight. Whenever it happened, sleep fled from his eyes, or it took him a while to fall asleep.

David felt a strong ache to speak to someone, anyone who would understand. *God, please help me.* Jasmine's face flashed before his eyes. She'd always understood him in the past—that was one of the things he'd loved about her. But he hadn't told her about Heather. How would she feel about it? It wasn't an easy topic to broach. And it was already very late. She would be fast asleep by now. But something assured him she would understand.

David jumped out of bed and exchanged his night clothes for a pair of jeans and a T-shirt. He grabbed the keys to his truck, his phone and wallet, and sprinted out of the apartment before he had a chance to change his mind.

CHAPTER 30

Jasmine heard her phone ringing as if from a distance. She stretched out her hand to search for it on the bedside table and swiped the answer button once she had it. "Hello," she answered in a sleepy voice.

"Jasmine, did I wake you?" a familiar voice asked.

Her eyes flipped open, and she checked the phone screen. She hadn't been dreaming. It was David.

"I'm sorry to wake you," he said.

"Is everything okay?" Jasmine asked as she sat up. David sounded different, like something was wrong.

"Sorry, I'll let you get back to sleep."

"Wait! Where are you?" Could it be he was outside? Jasmine raced to the window and looked out. Sure enough, she could make out David seated in his truck parked in front of her house. "Don't go anywhere. I'm coming down."

She ended the call and pulled a coat from her closet which she donned over the T-shirt and loose yoga pants she wore. What was wrong? He'd only been this way in the past when something major happened.

She left her room and went outside. The air was nippy, but she didn't really notice. All she was concerned about was David.

He stepped out of his truck as soon as he saw her. Jasmine walked up to him. His eyes looked tired, and he gave her a weak smile. "Hey, you," he said.

"Are you okay? What's wrong?" she asked as her eyes searched his.

Then David reached out and pulled her to him. His strong arms enveloped her and drew her in like he wanted his heart to be as one with hers. Warm, comfortable, like home she'd needed but never knew existed. His citrusy sandalwood scent filled her nostrils and warmed her insides like his arms did on the outside.

She snuggled closer, her arms moving of their own volition to encircle his back. She hoped her touch reached whatever it was that was troubling him and calmed him.

David let out a big sigh and pulled her in even further, resting his head on her shoulders and hanging unto her like she was his lifeline. They stayed that way for a few moments, and then his hold relaxed.

"I'm sorry—" he started saying.

"It's okay, I needed that too," she said. "Do you want to talk about it?"

He gave her a wry smile. "Why don't we sit in the truck? I can't have you catch a cold." He opened the passenger side for her, and she slid in. He walked around to the other side and did the same.

The truck's interior was warm and toasty, so Jasmine removed her coat. "I'm all ears," she said when she was done.

David swallowed and stared out the window for a moment. Then he started talking. "I had someone I was supposed to marry. Her name was Heather. We met when I had just begun my residency at UCLA. I was hurrying out of a coffee shop when I bumped into her and spilled coffee all over her dress. She was a lawyer and was on her way to the courthouse. Instead of getting mad at me, she just smiled and introduced herself. That's when I knew she was special. We ended up dating, and by the time I was finishing residency, I proposed to her and she agreed. We planned to get married the spring before I was supposed to start fellowship.

"We came home to Dexington for Christmas and it was the best holiday I ever had. We'd planned to stay in LA, but Heather brought up the idea of moving back to Dexington after my fellowship. She said I was much happier here, and she thought the town was pretty special too. It was close enough to Boston and New York to still keep her in touch with her kind of work. She was a corporate lawyer and could even work for us in our legal department or apply to Dexington Healthcare if she wanted. It was a great time, and then we travelled back to LA to continue planning for the wedding.

"That's when she started complaining that her stomach hurt. We thought it was nothing at first, but when she was still having the pains after a week, I insisted she see a GI doctor. It turned out she had cancer of the head of the pancreas." His voice cracked. "And only had three weeks to live."

Jasmine's heart dropped. That "C" word again. She could well imagine how he must have felt when he heard the news. His hand rested on the center console, and she reached out and placed hers over it.

He looked at her, his eyes twin mirrors of deep sorrow. "It was like my world ended," he said with a ragged voice. "I watched her wither away right in front of me, and I couldn't help her no matter what I did. There were nights I wanted to scream at the world, but I was afraid I would break down, and I had to be there for her even if I couldn't save her. She tried to remain upbeat even till the end, even when she was in so much pain. On the final day, she went into shock, and I watched them try to resuscitate her though it was in vain. My head knew she was gone, though my heart refused to acknowledge it.

"My world went dark. I don't know how I functioned. My parents flew into town and made all the funeral arrangements. She had no family—she'd survived and become who she was by pulling herself up by her boot straps. I could see her everywhere I turned and in everything around me. It was a miracle I completed my fellowship, because I did everything on auto-pilot. It became too much, and by the time I was finishing the program, I enlisted in the Army."

Jasmine's eyes filled with unshed tears at what David had gone through. She entwined her hand with his and waited for him to continue.

He stared straight ahead as he drew in a tremulous breath. "I was mad at God for weeks for taking her away and I told Him. Eventually, He calmed my soul as I worked hard to save each wounded soldier that was brought to my care. But I also watched men die who wished they'd had the chance to know love. That's when I realized He had given me the gift of knowing Heather before she'd left this earth. And I had memories that remained. The mug you broke at my house was the last gift she gave me before she died. That's why I was upset then." He gave her an apologetic smile.

Jasmine now understood. She would have been angry too if that happened to her.

"The pain of losing her has lessened over time, though I still miss her now and then. I used to have nightmares about her last moments regularly in the beginning, but I haven't had one in a while, until tonight. The emergency patient almost died on the table, and I think that's what triggered it."

They stayed silent for a few minutes.

Eventually, David turned and looked at her. "I'm sorry I dumped this on you. I've never really talked about it."

Jasmine gave him an encouraging smile. "Do you feel better?"

"I feel lighter. Thank you."

"You're welcome."

"It feels nice."

"What?"

"Holding your hand. I don't want to let go."

"Me neither."

"So what should we do?"

She looked out. The sky was still dark, a bit early in the morning. "How about we stay here for a while?"

"Are you sure? The truck is not exactly comfortable."

"It's fine."

"Okay. But we can recline our seats. That would be better."

Jasmine used her free hand to adjust her seat. David did the same. They turned on their sides, facing each other. Then his eyes fluttered closed and he fell asleep.

Jasmine watched the rise and fall of his chest. She felt her heart expand at the sight of this beautiful man that looked vulnerable and precious at the same time. A lock of his hair fell over his face, and she brushed it back. She traced the outline of the bridge of his nose—strong and masculine like she remembered.

She loved the part of him she had met today. Being vulnerable as a man was not a sign of weakness as far as she was concerned. But she wondered if he'd have room for her in his heart, given how much he'd loved Heather.

And now she worried how he would take her news. Would he be able to accept her, a cancer patient, when he'd lost his loved one to cancer? Still she had to tell him before they got too involved—it would feel like a betrayal otherwise. If he couldn't stay, it would be like a knife to her heart, but she would understand.

Her arm grew numb and she tried to pull her hand from his, but he held fast to it even though he was asleep. She adjusted her arm till she felt blood flowing again. She watched him for a few more minutes and then closed her eyes.

Dawn was around the corner.

It was time to catch some sleep.

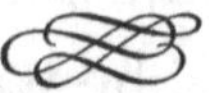

CHAPTER 31

David opened his eyes as the first rays of dawn rested on his eyelids. He felt refreshed, like he'd slept deeply, even though it had been in his truck. He noticed his hand was still entwined with Jasmine's.

He stared at her as she slept, her long eyelashes framing her face like delicate tendrils. Gosh, she was gorgeous. He could watch her all day. He still couldn't believe she was back in his life.

But she was more beautiful on the inside. He'd worried he might have offended her last night when he'd talked about another woman in her presence. But she hadn't judged him and had instead comforted him.

But he had to admit his feelings for her were now stronger than ever. There was just something about her that made him want to protect and keep her safe.

Her eyes fluttered open, first in confusion, and then a warm smile graced her face. "Hi, David," she said shyly.

David's heart skipped a beat. She had no idea what she was doing to him. She looked so tempting he wanted to kiss her silly. But this was not the right time. He didn't want her to think he'd done it in the heat of the moment, or like he was treating her as a replacement for Heather. "Hello, Jasmine. Welcome back," he said.

She laughed, the lyrical sound filling the air. David's heart skipped another beat. She would kill him at this rate if he wasn't careful.

"How are you feeling?" she asked him.

"I'm good. Thanks again for listening."

"My pleasure."

"So what's your plan for today?"

"I have a sleepover tonight at my roommate's in-law-to-be's house. It's for her wedding planning. A bunch of us are going to be there. You haven't met my roommates, have you?"

"No, I haven't."

"How about you pick me up this evening and drop me off at the venue? You'll get a chance to meet them at the same time."

"That would be fun. Is that okay, though? I don't want to interrupt any girly stuff."

Jasmine laughed. "Oh, there will be enough time for 'girly stuff' afterward."

"Okay. What time do you want me to pick you?"

"How about six p.m.?"

"That works."

"Great." Jasmine sat up. "I have to go in before my roommate, Dana, wonders if someone kidnapped me. I didn't bring my phone out."

She let go of his hand, and he felt the loss of her touch, like he was missing a piece of his arm. He jumped out of the truck and walked around to open her door for her. She hopped down, and he caught her. "Easy there," he said.

Electricity crackled between them at her nearness. His whole body hummed in response and his breath deepened. This was crazy, like his system had gone into overdrive.

Jasmine must have felt it too because she distracted herself by grabbing her coat from where it had fallen on the ground. "I have to go in," she said without meeting his eyes.

But he couldn't let her go just like that. He pulled her into a gentle embrace and then planted a soft kiss on her forehead. "I'll see you later," he said.

He let her go, and she stepped onto the sidewalk. David motioned for her to go in. She gave him a quick wave before entering her house and shutting the door behind her.

David climbed into the truck and drove away.

But he felt like he'd left a piece of his heart behind.

CHAPTER 32

David stopped the truck next to another parked car at the top of the long winding driveway that led to a stately brick mansion. "What does your roommate's fiancé do for a living?" he asked Jasmine.

"Because of the house?"

"Yes, it's massive."

"He's a medical resident," Jasmine said as she got out of the truck.

David did the same, but he also grabbed Jasmine's overnight bag from the backseat. "You are kidding, right?"

"No, I'm not." David gave her a disbelieving look. "But he is also the heir to Dexington

Healthcare." Dexington Healthcare was a conglomerate of health care businesses that included Dexington Medical Center where David and Jasmine worked.

"You mean Blake Dexington?"

"Yes. This is his family house." Jasmine led David to the front entrance of the home. "His mom is the one hosting the sleepover. Have you met him before?"

"I don't think so."

"He might be here. I'll introduce you."

Jasmine heard a buzz and a click from the large double French doors that graced the entrance as they approached. "There must be a security camera around here somewhere," David said.

"I'm sure."

David pulled open one of the doors and they stepped into a large cavernous foyer that then led to one of the most stunning living rooms that Jasmine had ever seen. It never failed to take her breath away each time she came here, and today was no exception. A large winding staircase served as the centerpiece of the huge living room which boasted multiple sets of French doors and large windows, an ornate fireplace and mosaic-tile floors. The rest of the furnishings had a designer signature touch to them.

"Aunt Jasmine!" Jasmine looked to her left to see a whirlwind with blonde hair racing toward her.

Jasmine grinned. She loved this precocious little eight-year old. "Willow!" She swept her up in her arms. "I've missed you!" Her hair had settled into long bangs that framed her cute face.

"I've missed you too, Aunt Jasmine. But can you put me down?"

Jasmine laughed and set her down.

Willow looked up at David. "Is this your boyfriend, Aunt Jasmine? He's cute!"

Jasmine laughed. Trust Willow to state the obvious. She'd had a crush on Josh, Dana's fiancé, a while ago until he'd gotten engaged. Now it seemed David would be the new one.

She turned to him. "David, meet Willow, princess extraordinaire."

David took Willow's hand and kissed the back. "Nice to meet you, Willow," he said with a bow.

Willow giggled. "I like him," she said to

Jasmine. She turned back to David. "Can I call you Uncle Dave?"

"Sure." David said and gave her a wink.

Willow turned red, and she covered her face. This was a new one. She'd never seen Willow blush.

"Hey, Jasmine." Blake Dexington walked up to where they stood, dressed in a white and blue polo shirt and chinos. "Hi, I'm Blake Dexington," he said and extended a hand to David.

David shook it in return. "David Landi."

"Of Landilis Silicone?"

"You know the company?"

"We've done some business with your father before. Are you the plastic surgeon?"

"Yes."

"Welcome back." At David's questioning look, "We heard about you from Professor Crouch. He was very keen on hiring you. How are you finding Dexington?"

"I haven't had time to explore the city since I got back."

"Well, we should stay in touch. I like to organize get-togethers from time to time. Any friend of Jasmine's is a friend of ours." He handed David a card. "Here's my number."

David pulled out a card from his wallet and gave his to Blake. "It was nice meeting you, Blake."

"Me too. I think I can hear the rest of the gang coming, which means it's time for me to get out of their hair. See you some other time, David." He held out a hand to Willow. "Come on, princess. Let's go bother Grandpa."

Willow took his hand and gave David a wave with the other. "Bye bye, Uncle Dave." David waved back in return.

"She's cute." David said to Jasmine.

"Yes, she is. She's Alicia's daughter, and Blake's family adores her."

"Jasmine! So good to see you again. Sorry we couldn't meet you at the door. The wedding dresses just arrived and we were taking a look." Blake's mom, Sarah Dexington walked over to where Jasmine stood, followed by Alicia and Dana.

"Good evening, Mrs. Dexington."

"It's Aunt Sarah. Mrs. Dexington is taking a nap and should be down soon. How are you, Jasmine?" Aunt Sarah turned to David. "And who is this fine young man?"

"I'm good. This is David Landi, a friend of mine."

"More like her boyfriend, Aunt Sarah," Dana chimed in.

Jasmine's ears turned red. Dana grinned.

"David Landi? Are you Elisa's son? I've done some charity work with her."

"Yes, ma'am."

"Please extend my greetings to her when you see her."

"I will, ma'am."

"I'm Alicia. This is Dana. It's nice to meet you," Alicia said with a smile.

David smiled back at them. "Same here. You all work at Dexington Medical Center, right?"

"Yes. Blake, Alicia, Josh, my fiancé, and myself are all residents there," Dana said. "Josh and I are surgical while Blake and Alicia are medical."

"Will you be staying?" Aunt Sarah asked.

"No, I just came by to drop Jasmine off, and I need to be on my way. It was nice meeting you all."

"Feel free to come by anytime. We welcome any friends of Blake's and Alicia's."

"Thank you, ma'am. Have a good day."

"I'll see him out," Jasmine said to Alicia and Dana.

They walked back through the foyer and out to the driveway.

"So what do you think?" Jasmine asked.

"Everyone was nice and welcoming. I liked it."

"They really are."

"Do you want me to come back and pick you up when you are done?"

"No need. Alicia will drop Dana and me off tomorrow. But I'll text you before I sleep."

David pulled her into his embrace. "Have fun, okay?"

She was liking these hugs. "I will."

David released her. "See you later." He strode to the truck and hopped in. Jasmine gave him a wave as he started the truck and drove down the driveway. He waved right back before he disappeared from view.

Jasmine walked back into the house.

"Oooh!" Alicia and Dana shouted in unison as they grabbed her arms and dragged her into the living room. Aunt Sarah was nowhere to be seen. They ended up on the couch.

Jasmine's ears grew warm. "Hey, cut it out."

"You didn't tell me he was Dr. McDreamy," Alicia said. "It seems I've been out of the loop. Spill!"

"Well, I found out Tony Landi and David Landi were the same person, and there had been a misunderstanding. You were right, Alicia, about keeping an open mind."

Alicia beamed. "Glad I could help. So is he your boyfriend?"

"Well, he asked me out and I said yes. But I'm not sure yet. There are just some things I need to figure out. He's a good person, so that's not the problem."

"Well, just make sure you pray about them," Dana said.

"I will. Now, I've heard the dresses have arrived. What about the wedding planner?"

"She had an emergency and needed to leave," Alicia said. "I'll call her later to make sure everything is alright."

"Okay. So what are we doing now?" Jasmine asked.

"It's time to get stuffed," Alicia said. "Blake's mom has outdone herself. We'll start trying the dresses on after dinner."

"Oooh! You look wonderful, Alicia," Aunt Sarah said. They were seated in a large parlor with a pedestal—where Alicia now stood—placed in the center of the room and a large mirrored room divider surrounding it to provide angled views of the dress. Racks filled with stunning wedding and bridesmaid dresses occupied one side of the room. "Do you think this might be the one?"

Alicia wiped tears from her eyes. "This is the one."

"You look fantastic, dear," Grandma Helen Dexington said. She had come down for dinner and had kept them in stitches the whole time.

Aunt Sarah got up and gave Alicia a hug. "I know you wish your sister and mom were here to see this." Alicia's mom and sister had died a few years ago.

Alicia nodded. "But I'm glad you and Grandma are here especially with Carol out of the country." Carol had been Alicia's sister's best friend and had checked in regularly with Alicia since her sister passed away in a car accident. "And you guys too." She nodded at Dana and Jasmine.

Unbidden tears filled Jasmine's eyes. Alicia looked so beautiful and radiant, exactly as a bride should, and she had met Blake, a wonderful man who loved her with all his heart. And Dana was headed down that road too. A sharp pain stabbed her heart. But she, Jasmine, would never get the chance. Not with this horrible cancer that had ruined her life. An involuntary sob escaped from her.

Grandma Helen, who was closest to her, pulled her into her arms. "What's wrong, honey?" she asked.

Jasmine sobbed louder. It was like a dam within her had broken, and she couldn't hold it back. Everything seemed too much for her. She wailed.

"Oh, dear God." Aunt Sarah rushed to her side and rubbed her back. Dana and Alicia also hastened to where she sat. "Shh. It's going to be alright."

"Let it all out, sweetheart," Grandma Helen said as she continued to hug her.

Jasmine rested her head on Grandma Helen's shoulder and cried. It was like all the hurt, pain, and hopelessness she'd bottled inside were determined to make their way out. And they flowed and flowed out till she had nothing else in her. Till her insides felt so empty and drained. And Grandma Helen, Aunt Sarah, Alicia, and Dana just surrounded her in a warm embrace.

Jasmine finally lifted up her head and wiped her tears between sniffles. Grandma Helen handed her a handkerchief. "Thanks," Jasmine said as she accepted it.

"Now, dear, you have to tell us what's wrong," Grandma Helen said.

Jasmine blew her nose before speaking. She could tell it was time. "I have cancer."

"Oh, dear Jesus," Aunt Sarah said. Jasmine could feel the ripple of shock make its way around the room.

"When did you find out?" Alicia asked quietly.

"Last week. I found a lump in my breast the night before I came back from the New York trip. The biopsy results came back last Friday."

"Why didn't you tell us?" Alicia asked. "You shouldn't have carried the burden alone."

"I didn't want it to color your wedding planning. It's not good news, and you both deserve worry-free weddings."

Alicia cupped Jasmine's face. "You're my sister. You are much more important to me." Tears welled up again in Jasmine's eyes and spilled down her face. "Hey, don't cry." Alicia wiped the tears away. "How bad is it?"

"They think it hasn't spread yet."

"That's good news. So they"ll just remove the lump, right?" Aunt Sarah asked.

"It's more than that. I have the BRCA mutation gene, so the best option is a double mastectomy."

"What's that?" Grandma Helen asked.

"The chance of a breast and/or ovarian cancer recurring is high for those who have the gene, so it's best to remove the breast tissue completely," Dana explained.

"Did they check the ovaries?" Alicia asked.

"There's nothing there so far. And there is some family history of breast cancer and not of ovarian, so they think the chances for that are less. But I'll have chemotherapy after the surgery to cover all the bases."

"You must have been scared," Aunt Sarah said as she rubbed Jasmine's back.

Jasmine thought for a moment. "I don't think it had fully sunk in. But when I saw Alicia in that dress, it dawned on me I may never get a chance to experience that."

"Why not, honey?" Grandma Helen said. "You think a man won't love you because you don't have breasts? Please! These jiggles go flat as a pair of slippers eventually. My Alex still thinks I'm sexy with mine."

"Grandma!" Alicia and Dana said in unison.

Jasmine chuckled. TMI. Grandma Helen never disappointed.

"If a man truly loves you, he'll stay through thick and thin," Aunt Sarah confirmed. "You don't have to be perfect. I can tell you that from experience."

"Me too," Alicia said.

"Me three," Dana said. They all laughed.

"Does David know?" Dana asked after the laughter had died down.

"Who's David?" Grandma Helen inquired.

"Her boyfriend," Alicia answered.

"He is not," Jasmine clarified.

"Why not?" Grandma Helen asked. "Is it because of the cancer?"

"He doesn't know yet."

"You should tell him," Aunt Sarah said. "Are you afraid he will leave you?"

"I had planned to tell him, but I just found out he lost someone he loved to cancer."

"That's the more reason why you should tell him," Aunt Sarah said. "He'll stay if he's the one for you. If not, God will bring the right person to you."

"And it's better you tell him sooner rather than later," Dana said. "You know he'll hear about it in the hospital—the surgical department is such a small world. It's best he hears it from you."

"I agree," Alicia said.

"Okay, I'll do that," Jasmine confirmed.

"What about your mom? Does she know?"

"I don't want to tell her yet. She'll freak out and blame herself for passing the gene to me."

"You should tell her," Grandma Helen said. "You might be surprised how she reacts. Mothers are lionesses when it comes to their babies."

"I'll think about it, Grandma," Jasmine replied.

"So." Grandma Helen let go of Jasmine and leaned back on the couch. "Are you getting a new pair of jiggles?" she asked with a twinkle in her eye.

Jasmine chuckled. "I plan to."

"Do they have colored ones? Rainbows? A red flaming pair to match your hair?"

The whole room erupted in laughter.

Jasmine felt a lightness in her heart as she looked around the room at the people who had adopted her as a sister, daughter, and granddaughter. She hadn't realized how heavy the burden of the cancer had been weighing down on her.

"You are going to be just fine, Jasmine Banks," Grandma Helen said. "And we'll be here for you. But most importantly, God is right by your side through it all."

"Amen," everyone chorused.

Jasmine's eyes shone with unshed tears.

She truly wasn't alone.

And it felt great.

The rest of the slumber party had gone off without a hitch. There had been lots of laughter, and singing may have found its way in there. Willow had joined them and oohed and aahed over Alicia's dress, which transformed to a shorter frock for the reception. Jasmine and Dana had both chosen a short V-necked A-line lace dress—Dana's in pale blue paired with a grey ribbon and Jasmine's in soft grey matched with a pale blue ribbon, to coordinate with Alicia's wedding colors. Willow's dress would be a mini replica of Alicia's.

The group had then relocated to a massive bedroom on the first floor that had been converted into one giant sleeping area. They were served nightcaps of freshly baked cookies and hot chocolate. The guys—Grandpa Alex, Blake's dad, and Blake—had dropped by to wish them goodnight but had been shooed away by Grandma Helen. Josh had been on-call, so he hadn't joined them.

By the time they were ready to fall asleep, it was too late to call David. So Jasmine sent him a quick text wishing him goodnight. David called back immediately.

"Hi," Jasmine said as she made her way out of the room to a small seating area on the first floor. "Did I wake you?"

"No," David replied. "I was waiting for your text before going to bed."

Jasmine's heart warmed at his words. "What if I hadn't sent the text?"

"I would have waited all night."

Her stomach fluttered, and she smiled. So cheesy. How could he say such nice words with a straight face?

"So how was the sleepover?" he asked.

"It was so much fun. Blake's Grandma is hilarious. She's someone you should meet."

"I'm glad you had a great time."

Jasmine remembered she had promised to tell David about the cancer. "How does your schedule look tomorrow?"

"I have to be at the hospital for most of the day. I need to make up for all the time I was out. Why do you ask?"

Though she'd have preferred tomorrow, it could wait. She still had a little time. "I just wanted to know."

"Are you missing me already? Can't stay away?" he teased.

Jasmine chuckled as she tucked her legs under her. "You are so full of yourself."

"Why not? I'm very lovable."

"Oh, geez. Is that what the nurses told you?"

"Don't tell me you're jealous of them. It's a blessing to have a face that brightens their day. Though that's an emotion I'd welcome very much from you."

"Really?"

"Yes, the same way I wouldn't want any guy hitting on you."

"You're nuts."

"I'm nuts over you."

Jasmine couldn't stop the corners of her lips from turning up into a smile. "Why does that sound like a lyric?"

"It might be."

She laughed. "Are you writing again?"

"It's a secret."

"I'd love to hear it sometime."

"Maybe if you give me a kiss."

"David!"

"A kiss for a song. Not bad, eh?"

Jasmine grinned. "I'll think about it."

"That's my girl."

She chuckled. "Are you okay, David? Are you sure you are not running a fever?"

"If I tell you, would you come and check on me, Doctor?"

Jasmine shook her head in disbelief and grinned. Was this the same David she knew? "I think it's time you headed to bed."

"I'm already in bed, baby."

She laughed. He would never stop. "Goodnight, David."

"Sweet dreams, darling."

CHAPTER 33

David chuckled as he dropped his phone beside him on the bed. He couldn't believe how playful and silly he'd been on the phone with Jasmine. She brought out this side of him he didn't know he still had. It had been like wooing her.

And maybe that was what he was doing. He'd planned to be careful and take his time in getting to know her again, but all that had disappeared when he'd heard her voice. There was just something magical about the way it touched him on the inside. And he hadn't wanted the call to end—he could have talked to her all night if possible.

He turned and lay on his side. He was more

excited and alive than he'd ever been in the last few years. It was like Jasmine was awakening every cell of his heart that he'd thought had died. He was now seeing colors instead of the gray and black that had dominated his life since Heather passed on. And he hadn't thought about Heather at all the whole time.

Had his heart accepted it was time to move on? Maybe it had been waiting for Jasmine. Was this God's plan all along in bringing him back to Dexington at this time? David had wanted no relationship, but God knew what he needed better than he did. His heart seemed happy for it.

But something nagged at the back of his mind. Like a puzzle he needed to figure out. What was it? He racked his brain. Yes, Jasmine had mentioned she had something to tell him when he'd asked her out. Come to think of it, she'd brought it up again at their date.

He sat up and leaned against the headboard. Hmmm. What was it that was so important she had to tell him? He'd said it didn't matter, which he still stood by, but maybe he needed to hear her out.

What could it be? Did she have a child? That

wouldn't be a big deal, and he loved kids anyway. But she would have mentioned it when she'd told him about Alicia's daughter. Was it a boyfriend? No way! Jasmine would have told him upfront and refused to date him—she wasn't the cheating type.

Or could she be sick? She looked pretty healthy to him, but then appearances could be deceiving—he'd learned that with Heather. *God, please, don't let that be it.*

Because he wasn't sure if his heart could survive such an experience again.

CHAPTER 34

*J*asmine stifled a yawn as she stepped out of the ER cubicle in her blue scrubs and white coat. She'd ended up spending so much of Sunday with Alicia and Dana that she hadn't gotten enough sleep by the time she'd finished the mountain of work that had awaited her that evening.

She'd gotten into the hospital early as usual on Monday, but it had been very busy so far, with two newly admitted patients with serious complications and three back-to-back surgeries. She'd just finished attending to a fifty-year-old patient that had arrived with significant uterine bleeding from massive fibroids. They'd managed to stabilize her and had scheduled her for a hysterectomy the next day.

Jasmine had also called Prof. Morgan and told her about the cancer. Prof. Morgan had been upset but had reassured Jasmine she'd get through this. She'd approved Jasmine's medical leave and had promised to have someone ready on Wednesday to take over her patient load.

She turned her neck from side to side. She needed a break. Jasmine still had a long way to go before signing off for the day. She wasn't really hungry, but maybe it made sense to grab something to eat as well.

She left the ER and headed down the empty hallway. She'd make a stop at the cafeteria and then sneak in a fifteen-minute nap at the resident on-call room, before heading upstairs to the ICU to make sure her post-op patients were doing okay.

A hand grabbed hers out of nowhere, and Jasmine turned. It was David, in blue scrubs with a stethoscope around his neck. He gave her a lazy grin.

Her heart skipped a beat. Ah, the one face she could never get tired of seeing. She smiled. "Hey, where did you come from?" she asked.

"I just finished with a patient in the ER." He led her down the hallway, still holding her hand. Jasmine hurried to follow.

"Me too. Where are we going?"

"You'll see."

They reached the surgical attending on-call room, and David pushed the door open.

"David, I shouldn't be here," Jasmine said.

The somewhat large room was empty—the twin beds and small conference table were unoccupied.

David closed the door behind them and pulled her into a hug. Sparks of electricity zapped through her as his skin touched hers. And gosh, he smelled good.

"I've missed you," he said. "I needed this."

She snuggled deeper into his arms, and her eyes searched his face. He had circles around his eyes. "Have you been here since yesterday?" she asked with concern.

"More or less. I went home early this morning to freshen up before coming back. And I had a long microsurgery this morning. It's been a while since I used the equipment, so I guess I'm more tired than usual. But I'm glad I ran into you. You look beautiful." He smiled, and the left dimple that drove her crazy appeared.

And in that moment, all she wanted to do was kiss him. Kiss that dimple or those lips. But would David kiss her back? She had to find out.

She turned her face up, and her fingers brushed his silken hair as her arms looped around the back of his neck, drawing him close. Gosh, he was beautiful, with his strong jaw lines and the gold flecks in his eyes that burned like fire. His breath feathered her cheek, his citrusy sandalwood scent enveloping her as he met her halfway. He tilted her chin, the touch of his hand sending sparks through her skin. And then her lips met his.

Butterflies exploded and danced in her belly as he kissed her back. His lips were soft, sweet, just like she'd imagined, and she loved his minty taste. And then he kissed her hard, stealing her breath, devouring her lips like he couldn't get enough of her. A little gasp caught in her throat. She loved this side of him too.

He dug his fingers into the back of her hair till the hair tie holding up her ponytail fell off, and her hair cascaded in waves around her face. The butterflies in her stomach went into a frenzy, and she locked her arms behind his neck, deepening the kiss. It was like the kiss had reenergized her, and she wanted more.

"Ahem, sorry, I didn't ... I'll go grab lunch," an unfamiliar voice said.

Jasmine flinched and hid her face in the crook of David's neck. She hadn't heard the door open. This was so embarrassing. She was afraid to turn and see who it was.

The door closed, and then David held her away from him to look at her face. "Are you okay?" he asked.

"I'm fine," she said as she stepped away from his arms. "I need to go."

"Jasmine—"

She smiled at him. "I enjoyed the kiss. It's just ..." She noticed a somewhat familiar folded document on the floor by his feet.

David followed her gaze and picked it up before she could. "What is this?" he asked, his face changing from amusement to shock on flipping it open.

Jasmine froze. She'd forgotten the pre-op document she'd picked up from Dr. Allen's office manager this morning had been in her coat pocket. It had probably fallen out during their kiss.

"Jasmine?" David's face was ashen. "Isn't this for a surgery?"

Jasmine sighed. She guessed there was no better time than now to tell him the truth. She might just lose the best thing that had ever happened to her. But there was no running from it. If it ended the relationship, so be it.

"It's what I've been wanting to tell you. David, I have breast cancer."

CHAPTER 35

David felt a sudden coldness hit his body, like he was being sucked into a chilling vortex. Cancer? Jasmine had cancer? Could she really be talking about cancer after they'd just shared the best kiss ever? He shook his head. No way. It had to be a dream.

His hand clutched the pre-op papers so tight that it hurt. Ouch! This was real. He stared at her. His beautiful Jasmine had cancer. It was Heather all over again.

He broke out in a cold sweat and felt panic rising up within him. His heart raced as if to bolt out of his chest, and he couldn't get enough air in his lungs. But he forced himself to remain upright. No, he couldn't fall apart now. *Get it together, David, she needs you.*

He closed his eyes and struggled to take deep breaths as he fought the desire to run away and never experience the hurt, despair, and brokenness again. *God, help me. I can't do this alone.*

That was when he felt his lungs opening up and flooding with oxygen. He could breathe again. And then his heart rate began to slow its frantic pace. *Thank you, God.*

David opened his eyes. His beautiful Jasmine still stood there, waiting with a resigned look on her face. But if she thought he was going to abandon her, then she had another think coming. He'd left her once when she needed him, but he hadn't known then. This time around would be different. It didn't matter if his knees buckled at the thought of going through this hell again—he would be here for her. He wasn't going anywhere.

A strong protectiveness for Jasmine overcame him. David reached out and wrapped her in his arms. A sob escaped from her, and she held onto him tightly. Sweet beautiful Jasmine. She must have been so scared. "It's going to be okay," he said. And while she cried some more, he held her and prayed silently. For strength, for grace, for peace, and for joy to get through this. He felt God's peace fill his heart, and he knew they would be okay no matter the outcome.

It wasn't going to be easy. There would be times when he would be discouraged, when he would get mad at God again. But he could get through this. He had God on his side to hold him up, no matter what the result at the end was.

When Jasmine's tears were all spent, David lifted her face and wiped her tears away. "We will fight through this together," he said. He led her to the conference table and pulled out a chair for her. "Now tell me everything you know."

And Jasmine told him about the lump, the BRCA gene mutation, her family history, the pathology results, and the scheduled surgery on Thursday. "I had planned to tell you and kept looking for the perfect time," she said. "But then you told me about Heather, and I lost all courage."

He brushed an errant strand of hair away from her face. "I'm here now. You won't go through this alone, okay?" She gave him a small smile in return. "I'll take Thursday off to be with you."

"You can't. You just got back."

"I'll be fine. I can always make it up another day. But everyone is going to find out we're dating when they see me by your side. It doesn't bother me, but I don't want to put you in an awkward position. Is that okay?"

"I'll have to deal with it. It was going to happen anyway."

"Okay. Will your mom be there as well on Thursday?"

"No, I haven't told them about the cancer yet, and I'd like to keep it that way. My mom would be devastated, and it would be too much for me to handle right now. I plan to tell her after the surgery. But Alicia and Dana know."

"Alright." He reached for her hand and kissed it. "It's going to be fine."

She gave him a wry smile. "I'm sorry for being such a mood killer."

A smile tugged at the corners of his lips. "Who said the mood was dead? I can totally reignite it."

She laughed, the musical note filling the air.

"You're sure? Let's see what you can do, Doctor," Jasmine said with a twinkle in her eye.

And who was he not to oblige? David leaned forward and gave her a kiss that he hoped reassured her—one full of hope and a promise that he'd always be there for her.

He was going to stand by her side and help fight this cancer.

Because she was worth it.

CHAPTER 36

Jasmine walked through the double doors that led to the offices where the afternoon clinic was going to take place. She reached her assigned office, entered, and sat down. It was going to be a busy Tuesday afternoon; the waiting room she'd passed was full.

She'd heard the whispers as she'd headed here. The news about her relationship with David had already spread throughout the hospital. Jasmine was sure it was courtesy of David's colleague who had seen them together yesterday.

She'd noted the surprised gazes from her colleagues—Jasmine had never dated anyone in the hospital since attending medical school here. A few had congratulated her on her quick uptake, but they had no idea that Jasmine and David had a history. Some nurses had even given her the stink eye—maybe because she'd snatched up their darling Dr. Landi before they'd had a chance to make a move.

But Jasmine wasn't worried about any of it. She and David had not violated any ethics code. One good thing had come out of it though. She didn't have to worry about them seeing David by her side on Thursday.

Her medical assistant, Theresa, a young Bostonian with short wavy dark hair, entered the office, and they exchanged quick pleasantries before her first patient came in. Thirty-two-year-old Marsha Finch had been a patient of theirs for the past nine months. She'd been diagnosed with breast cancer with the BRCA gene just like Jasmine and had undergone a double mastectomy plus adjuvant chemotherapy. She was here for her bi-yearly checkup. Jasmine had seen her before, and they had bonded based on their shared love for the thrills.

"How are you doing today, Ms. Finch?" Jasmine asked as she gestured for her to sit down. Marsha was a lithe woman with short blond curls who had been a marathon runner before she'd found out about the cancer.

Marsha rubbed her eyes. "I don't know."

"What's going on?" Jasmine asked softly.

Marsha looked at Theresa and said nothing. It seemed Marsha would prefer to speak in private, so Jasmine asked her to excuse them for a few minutes. Theresa gave Marsha a reassuring smile and then left.

Marsha leaned back into her seat and let out a sigh. "It's my boyfriend. We'd been going out for three years and were about to tie the knot when we found out I had cancer. We postponed the wedding so I could focus on my treatment, and he promised he would be there for me. But then he told me yesterday that everything was too much for him. That he was breaking up with me. He could no longer deal with the fear that the cancer might come back or I might die. That it wasn't what he'd signed up for."

"I'm so sorry to hear that, Marsha."

Marsha took a deep inhale and exhale. "I'm glad I found out now instead of after the wedding, but it still hurts. He'd promised we'd fight through this together. But here am I, all alone. It feels so discouraging."

"I'm sorry it didn't work out. Have you considered attending our breast cancer support group? They meet at lunch time on Fridays. It's a great group; I've attended a couple of times. They even have scheduled times for venting and for celebrating milestones."

"Really? I haven't been to it."

"Okay, I'll make a note for the office manager to give you more details about it. Sometimes we just need the support of those who understand what we're going through."

"That would be great."

"Otherwise, how are you doing?"

They talked through her progress, and Jasmine examined her. She wrote down her notes and then brought in the attending to review Marsha's case. Theresa came back in then and Jasmine handed the orders to her.

The rest of the clinic went by quickly. Soon, all the patients had been seen. A few had been admitted, and those with upcoming surgeries had their pre-op interview scheduled with the anesthesiologist.

Jasmine leaned back as the last patient left

the room. What Marsha told her lingered on her mind. Marsha and her boyfriend had been far into their relationship, yet he'd deserted her. So how did that bode for Jasmine? She and David had not made any commitments to each other. What if it became too much for him and he left her?

No way. She was probably worried for nothing. David was a man of his word. He would never abandon her.

But then she couldn't shake the uneasy feeling that things might not go as planned.

Her phone vibrated at that moment. Jasmine picked it up and answered it. "Jasmine Banks," she said.

"Good afternoon, Dr. Banks. This is Wendy from Dr. Allen's office."

"Hello, Wendy."

"Dr. Banks, unfortunately, I have to inform you that your surgery with Dr. Allen has been postponed."

Jasmine sat up. This couldn't be happening. "Postponed? Why?"

"Dr. Allen is out on an emergency leave and won't be able to handle any cases in the near future. The next available spot is in two months when he will be back. Would that work?"

Two months could mean so much in the world of cancer including a transition from life to death. "Can't we get an earlier date?"

"The only availability we have is in two weeks with another breast surgeon in the service. But he's only able to handle the mastectomy; Dr. Allen is the only one board-certified in both fields. We'll need a reconstructive surgeon to join him. But none is available in the next three months, except for Dr. Landi, who we've just heard is a potential family member, which disqualifies him."

So, the rumor about their relationship had reached Wendy's ears. Still, there was no way Jasmine would have allowed David to handle the surgery, even if no one knew about them. It would have been too traumatizing for him.

"Alright, I'll take the two-month spot, but please keep me in mind if anything comes up."

"Thank you for your kind understanding. Have a good day." The line went dead.

Jasmine rested her head on the table. This was terrible. She couldn't imagine worrying about this lump and cancer for the next two months. It had been one thing after another. Couldn't she catch a break?

She needed to vent.

She picked up her phone and speed-dialed a number.

CHAPTER 37

"I'm so upset, David. I know it's not Dr. Allen's fault, but I don't know what to do."

"I heard he was in an accident," David said. "But still, you have every right to be mad about the change," David responded quietly. He'd ended his surgery for the day and had just returned to his office before Jasmine called.

"Now I feel even worse, like I'm throwing a tantrum," Jasmine responded.

David's hand twiddled with his pen as he sat facing the window. "It's okay to feel gutted. This is a life and death scenario."

"I could have the surgery in two weeks, but only if I split the reconstruction from the mastectomy. I really don't want to have two separate surgeries if I can help it. And I'm afraid of how I'd feel with no breasts. Is that so vain of me?"

"No. They've been a part of you for a long time, and it can be devastating to lose them at once."

"I know. I try not to think too much about it, but I feel the breast implants would help me deal better with their loss. But on the other hand, I worry if delaying the surgery by two months would be worth it, given the combined surgery comes with its own set of complications. Aargh, I don't know what to do."

"It's going to be alright, Jasmine. And it's not a betrayal to cancer survivorship if you want new breasts immediately. But know that you'll always be beautiful to me no matter what choice you make."

"Sorry, I know this is such a weird conversation to have, talking about breasts."

David smiled. "It's fine. Have you forgotten I talk about them all the time with patients who need reconstruction? Definitely not weird for me. But don't go having this conversation with anyone else. I can assure you it would be awkward."

"By the way, did you know everyone knows about our relationship?"

"Oh, so that's what it was all about. Some of my colleagues were cracking some weird jokes. It's fine."

"What kind of jokes? Tell me."

"Something about catching a beautiful fish. I'm not really into fishing, so I didn't get it at the time. I had no idea you had so many admirers."

Jasmine laughed. "It's not my fault. I can't help it."

"It's good to hear you laugh. It's going to be alright, okay?"

"Thanks for letting me vent."

"No problem."

"I'll let you get back to work."

"You can call me anytime."

"Even when you're in surgery?"

"Yes, as long as you don't mind everyone overhearing our conversation."

"That would just be more fodder for the rumor mill. No way am I contributing to that!"

"As you wish, darling."

"Alright, bye." She ended the call.

David chuckled. He could never get tired of chatting with her.

His face turned serious. She must have been really upset to call about the postponement. He didn't want her to be more stressed than she already was. Maybe there was something he could do about it.

He picked up his phone and dialed a number from memory. The person on the other end of the line answered the call. "Hello, this is Karen Lee." Prof. Karen Lee was one of the best reconstructive surgeons in the US and had extensive experience with the combined mastectomy-reconstructive surgery.

"Hi, Karen, it's David Landi."

"David! I heard you were back stateside and at Dexington. How are you?"

"Good. I called your number the weekend I came back, but your voicemail was full."

"Sorry. I saw the missed call from a strange number, and you know how I am with those."

"No worries."

"So what's going on? I'm sure you didn't call during working hours to chitchat."

"I need a huge favor."

"Go on."

"I have a friend who was scheduled to have a combined mastectomy-reconstructive surgery on Thursday, and now the surgeon is no longer available. I was wondering if you could fly in and take care of it. I remembered you had a license to practice in this state."

"I still do. Let me check my schedule." David could hear mouse clicks in the background.

Karen came back on the line. "Okay, my calendar is relatively open for that day, and I can move the rest of my appointments to other days. I can make it work. But I don't have hospital privileges at Dexington Medical Center, and you know the usual red tape."

"What if I took care of that? Would that work?"

"Only if you can get her surgeon to release access to her case files to me today."

"I can do that. I'll send my jet to pick you up."

"Get that sorted and we'll make it happen."

"Thanks! I'll get back to you shortly."

"Alright then. Talk to you soon." The line went dead.

David let out a sigh of relief. It was a miracle that Karen was willing to do this. *Thank you, God.* Now to take care of the red tape.

He pulled out the business card from his

wallet and called the number. The line rang twice and then he answered. "Blake Dexington speaking."

"Blake, it's me, David Landi."

"Hey, David. What's going on?"

"Would it be possible to get hospital privileges for a surgeon right away, as in today? It's important."

"Is it for Jasmine?"

"How did you know?"

"Alicia told me about the cancer. And I heard about Dr. Allen."

"I know a renowned surgeon from UCLA, Professor Karen Lee, who is willing to come in for Thursday, but you know the usual red tape. I was wondering if you could take care of that."

"Consider it done. Jasmine is family. And we've been trying to get Prof. Lee to come. Maybe this would be a good opportunity for us to try and poach her. I'll have my secretary send her the paperwork and copy you on it. I'll also get Dr. Allen to release access to her file."

"Thank you."

"Anytime. Feel free to reach out if you need anything else."

"I will. Have a good day."

"You too." The call ended.

This was awesome. He dialed back Karen's number.

"Hi, David."

"It's all set. You should get all the paperwork and the access to my friend's case file shortly."

"Wow, that was fast. She must be really special."

"She is. Thank you so much for doing this."

"My pleasure, David. Now, you owe me, and you know I always collect."

David laughed. "Oh, that I know very well."

"Talk to you later."

"Bye."

David dropped his phone on his desk. It was done. Jasmine could still have her surgery on Thursday. He would leave it to Dr. Allen's office manager to let her know when all the arrangements were finalized.

He was just happy he would be able put a smile on her face.

CHAPTER 38

Thursday morning dawned bright and early. David had already been up awhile, spending some of that time committing the surgery into God's hands. He'd taken the day off and was about to leave for the hospital. He'd offered to pick Jasmine up, but she'd declined, saying she preferred to head there alone. David understood. It must be hard knowing this was the day her life would change.

She'd been so excited and had called him after she'd heard the surgery was going ahead, though she'd wondered how it had happened. But he hadn't told her what he'd done. Some things were better left unsaid.

His phone rang as he picked up his car keys. He looked at the screen. It was Karen. She'd arrived late last night, and he'd made sure she was settled in the best hotel in town. He answered the call. "Good morning, Karen. I was just on my way to the hospital."

"David, we have a problem."

His heart sank. Was there something wrong with Jasmine's surgery? "What is it?"

"I just got a call that one of my old patients, Thelma Warren—I'm sure you remember her— needs an emergency pelvic floor reconstruction following a complication she had. She's refusing all the other doctors, saying she would only allow you or me to perform it, since we were her surgeons the first time. This one isn't expected to be as complex. But I can't go. Do you think it would be possible for you to fly to LA and do the surgery? They are willing to wait till you get there."

David groaned inwardly. It would mean not being by Jasmine's side, and she would be pissed. But he owed Karen, and Thelma Warren was special to her. Good thing his state license and hospital privileges were still current. "Okay, I'll head there."

David heard her quiet exhale. "Thanks, David. This means a lot. I'll give you access to her case files now and let the team know."

"Sounds good." He heard a call coming through. "I'll let you go."

"Good luck."

The line went dead, and he answered the incoming call. "David Landi."

"Hi, David. It's Alicia. I got your number from Blake."

"Hello. What's going on?"

"Are you going to be there for Jasmine today? I'd planned to be, but I just found out I need to head to Germany immediately to present a research paper. My colleague who was supposed to go just called in sick, and I've been asked to represent the team instead. Dana is on-call today, so she won't be there all the time, and Jasmine needs someone by her side."

"I'll take care of it. Don't worry. Just go ahead."

"Thank you so much."

"Have a safe trip."

"Bye." The call ended.

David pinched the bridge of his nose. At this point, there was only one choice. Jasmine was going to be mad when she found out, but it was the best call at this time.

David speed-dialed the number.

CHAPTER 39

Jasmine's eyes searched for David as she sat and waited to be called into the pre-op room. She'd checked in and had been given a patient band. There were a few other patients waiting as well with their family and well-wishers, but Jasmine sat alone. She'd seen two missed calls from David and had called him back but had gotten his voicemail instead.

Where was he? He'd promised he'd be here bright and early. She hadn't bothered to ask Alicia or Dana to come since she knew their schedules would be busy. But she'd expected David to be here by now.

Then she smelled a familiar coconut rose

scent waft its way to her nose. It couldn't be. Maybe there was someone else here who enjoyed the scent.

"Jasmine!" Jasmine looked up and saw her mom in a pink blouse and jeans standing a few feet away, concern written all over her face. Their eyes met, and Jasmine saw disbelief, grief, and then acceptance mirrored in her mom's. Her mom rushed forward and crushed Jasmine in her arms. "My poor baby." Jasmine could sense her making a mammoth effort not to cry.

"Mom, you are squeezing me."

Her mom released her. "Oh, sorry."

"What are you doing here?"

Jasmine's mom sat down beside her and brushed Jasmine's stray hair away from her face. "How could you not tell me, Jasmine? I felt like the biggest fool on earth when I heard about it. How could I have been sleeping soundly while my baby was going through this all alone?"

"I'm sorry, Mom. I didn't want you to feel guilty."

"How I feel isn't important. You are."

"I'm sorry."

"Come here." Her mom wrapped her arms

around Jasmine. "You'll be okay, dear. My baby's going to be alright."

Jasmine snuggled into her mom's arms. It was like the final weight had been rolled off. It felt so good to have her mom here. "What about dad?"

"I asked him not to come this morning. I didn't think it was a good idea if we both broke down. He'll come later in the evening once the surgery is over." She held Jasmine away from her. "Look at me. Those breasts are important, but they don't make you who you are. They were created to complement you and be a blessing in your life. Once they lose that function, it's totally fine to have them replaced with new ones, okay?"

Jasmine nodded. Her mom knew just what to say.

"You know what?" her mom said. "I think we should celebrate today henceforth as your breast birthday, the day your new implants arrive."

Jasmine chuckled. Trust her mom to come up with the most ridiculous ideas.

"I mean it," her mom insisted. "Happy breast birthday, Jasmine!"

Jasmine could feel all the curious stares directed at them. Her face warmed. "Mom, shh! You are too loud."

"Okay, okay. But we'll celebrate it. I'll tell your father to buy the cake on his way here in the evening."

"There you are." Jasmine looked up to see David's mom in a cute belted mauve dress heading toward them.

Jasmine looked at her mom. "Mom, did you tell her?"

"No. David called his mom, who then called me. That's how I found out."

The elusive David. But where was he? She was the only person that hadn't heard from him.

Elisa reached them. "Jasmine, I'm glad I caught up with you guys," she said.

"Hello, Mrs. Landi," Jasmine responded.

"How are you feeling? David told me what happened."

That big mouth. Where was he by the way?

"He's on his way to LA," David's mom answered as if she could read Jasmine's thoughts. "He said he tried your number but couldn't reach you."

"Yes, I saw those. Did he say what he was going for?"

Elisa shook her head. "No idea."

"Jasmine Banks?" a bespectacled nurse with a clipboard called out.

"I'm here," Jasmine responded.

The nurse compared the ID number she had with the one on the patient band that Jasmine wore. "Please follow me."

Jasmine and her entourage followed the nurse into a pre-op area similar to the one Jasmine was used to. It had multiple beds arranged around the room with a wall dedicated to lockers in which patients could store their belongings. Another set of doors led from the room to the operating theatre.

The nurse led Jasmine to a bed, helped her change into a hospital gown, checked her vitals, and set up an IV line. "Dr. Lee will be here shortly," she said before leaving.

"Dr. Jasmine Banks?" Jasmine looked up to see a striking young female surgeon with beautiful eyes that hinted at an Asian ancestry. "It's nice to meet you. I'm Dr. Karen Lee, and I'll be your surgeon for today. I'm sure you know the drill, but let's walk through it, okay?" She took

Jasmine through the final pre-op checklist and had Jasmine sign her consent for the surgery. "Do you have any questions for me?" she asked finally.

"None."

"Good. I can see why David is enamored with you."

Now, how did she know David?

"We've been close friends for a very long time," Dr. Lee said.

What did that even mean? "Okay."

She flashed a smile at Jasmine. "I'll see you in there. Good luck."

Before Jasmine could dwell on what had just transpired, the anesthesiologist came by and finished his pre-op check. Jasmine signed off on his consent form as well.

The nurse returned as the anesthesiologist was leaving. "We'll be taking you into the OR in a few minutes, okay?" Then she stepped away.

This was it. By the time she woke up, her world as she knew it would have changed. She wished David was here. And why had he broken his promise?

"It's going to be alright," David's mom said as she laid a reassuring hand on Jasmine's arm.

She'd stayed quiet the whole time the doctors had been present. Jasmine suspected she'd been praying.

Jasmine turned to ask her a question that had been bugging her. "Don't you find it upsetting that your son is interested in someone who has to deal with cancer and is about to lose her breasts?"

Elisa thought for a moment before she spoke. "It's not what I would have wished, I doubt anyone else would want that. But you're important to my son, which makes you important to me. And after what he went through with Heather, all I want for him is to be happy. And he's been smiling again since you came back into his life."

But where was he? Jasmine pulled out her phone and looked at the screen. No missed call.

"I'm sure it's something he couldn't get out of if he had to leave you to go to LA," his mom said. "Although, come to think of it, what's today's date?"

"The fifth," Jasmine said.

"It can't be."

"What is it?"

"Today is Heather's death anniversary. But that can't be the reason why he's there."

Jasmine felt like she'd been stabbed in her heart, and she almost doubled over.

"Are you okay?" her mom asked.

"I'm fine. I'm just nervous."

But it wasn't that. Had Jasmine been deceiving herself this whole time, thinking there was a place in David's heart for her?

Because truth be told, even though she had no idea when it'd happened, she, Jasmine Banks, had fallen hard for David Antonio Landi again. She loved this man with all her heart. So it was a hard pill to swallow if he didn't have space for her in his.

Could it be he'd tried but couldn't forget Heather, who would always remain number one in his life, and going through this with her was too much for him?

If that were the case, then maybe it was better to end their relationship now before she got more hurt.

CHAPTER 40

David stepped out of the OR wing and stretched his neck from side to side. The surgery was finally over. It had been good to work with the old team again. He'd kept his focus throughout, though it'd been a struggle, especially since he hadn't been able to reach Jasmine. All he wanted to do was head back to Dexington and be with her.

"David, it's so good to see you again." It was Prof. Pointe, his mentor, a white-haired bespectacled plastic surgeon that was legendary in the field of reconstructive surgery.

David shook his hand. "Great to see you too, Professor."

"How long are you in town?"

"I'm headed back to Dexington."

"So soon?" He studied David. "I can tell it's a woman from the look on your face."

David touched his face. Was there something on it?

Prof. Pointe laughed. "You look happy," he said. "It's great to see. I was always worried about you after what happened with Heather, and then when you took off to the Army … Anyway, it's good to see you relaxed and full of life, even more than when Heather was alive. You must love her then."

Was he in love with Jasmine? Was that why he found it hard to stay away from her?

"Don't let me keep you," Prof. Pointe said. "Make sure you stay in touch. And I want an invitation to the wedding." He strode off, giving David a wave above his head.

His mentor had always been able to read him more than anyone else. Now that he thought about it, Jasmine occupied his mind all the time. And even though she drove him crazy sometimes, he was happy being around her. She'd crashed through all of his walls, yet he felt comfortable and safe with her. And her happiness was important to him. It seemed Prof.

Pointe had just pointed out what his heart had been trying to tell him all along.

David felt a warmth spread from his heart through his body. He was in love with Jasmine Banks, that redheaded spitfire that had wormed her way into his heart. She'd done to him what he'd thought impossible after Heather's death.

He had to rush back to be with her.

But, first, he had one last thing to take care of before he could leave.

David stood and looked down at the headstone in front of him. He bent down and swept away the stray leaves that had fallen on it. The grounds around it were well-manicured—David had paid for year-round care of the place and always would. He knew she was no longer in the grave, that she was free of pain, resting in the arms of the Savior, and that this place was more of a memorial for him.

He would always carry a piece of her in his heart. She had been special to him, and he had loved and had been loved. And for that he would always be grateful. Now, God had given him the gift of another love, one he would cherish with all his heart.

"Heather, I just wanted to say goodbye. You told me to make sure I love again, but I always thought that would never happen." He chuckled. "Well, you proved me wrong, just like always. Her name is Jasmine, and she's a wonderful person. Because of the love you and I shared, you taught me to love hard as long as I had breath in me. Now, I can cherish her much more because of you. Thank you."

He removed the couple's rings he'd always worn on a chain around his neck since Heather passed away, made a small hole in the ground next to the headstone and buried the rings there.

"Goodbye, Heather."

He turned and walked away to the town car that would take him to his family jet at the airport.

It was time to head back to Dexington.

To a certain lady he had to declare his love to.

CHAPTER 41

Jasmine turned her face to look out the large window overlooking the grounds as she lay on the hospital bed. She felt so tired, and her whole body ached. The surgery had been a success, and there had been no complications so far. Her mom and David's mom had stayed the whole time and waited for her.

The surgery had lasted about six hours, and then she'd spent the next three in the recovery room. They had wheeled her back an hour ago to the VIP wing where Blake had reserved a room for her.

It had been great to wake up to see her parents, David's parents, Alicia, Blake, Dana, and Josh surrounding her bed. Even Aunt Sarah and Grandma Helen had stopped by. They'd joked and laughed so much that the nurses had threatened to send them all away.

Her father had appeared with the cake in tow. Jasmine had almost died with embarrassment when they'd sung a Happy Breast Day song for her. She'd been surrounded by so much more love than she'd ever imagined.

But the one person she'd longed to see the most had been absent. She'd lost count of the number of times she'd asked her mom if he'd called. He'd disappeared as if into thin air. And no matter how much his mom reassured her, her heart still ached from missing him. Had it been too hard for him to forget Heather and be with her through this? Was that why he'd abandoned her? Maybe it was best to let him go.

Everyone had eventually left except for her mom, who had gone to grab dinner with her dad. She would be back once she was done.

The door slid open behind her. Maybe it was her mom. Jasmine turned her head only to see David hastening to her bedside.

Was it really him or was it just a figment of her imagination?

Then his familiar citrusy sandalwood scent hit her nostrils, and she had no doubt he was really the one.

"Jasmine." He came by her side and held her hand. Her skin vibrated at his touch.

Jasmine's heart squeezed in pain. He had this much effect on her, yet he didn't love her, and that would eventually break her. She withdrew her hand from his.

"Jasmine, I'm so sorry for breaking my promise to be here," he said.

A part of her heart leaped at his voice, wanting to believe him. No! She had to protect herself, guard her heart from shattering to pieces. Because that was what would happen if she loved him and he didn't love her back.

"I have something to say," he said.

She had to stop this from going any further, no matter how much it hurt her to do so. "I have something to say too," she said.

"Okay, you go first."

"Did you go to Heather's grave?"

"How did you ...? Yes."

Jasmine's heart broke. So it was true. Heather was more important to him. She took a deep breath. She could do this no matter how much it hurt. "It's over between us."

His eyes widened. "What do you mean?"

"It's over, David. There can be nothing between us." She turned her face to avoid his eyes, those twin pools that drew her like a moth to a flame. "I want to be left alone."

"Jasmine—"

"Please leave, David," she said in a weary tone. She wasn't sure how much longer she could take his presence before she shattered.

David didn't say anything, just got up and walked out of the room, and out of her life.

Jasmine broke down and wept.

CHAPTER 42

Jasmine winced as she sat up on the couch. The drugs she'd been given at the hospital had worn off a few days ago, and the pain in her chest had returned with a vengeance. She'd refused the narcotics she'd been given and stuck instead with regular painkillers, which only took the edge off the pain. But each day had gotten better than the last.

She'd been discharged from the hospital, and her parents had insisted that they take her home. Her mom had practically waited on her hand and foot. The care had made a difference, and she was now moving on her own around the house. Everything was healing well.

Except for her heart—there was a hole there that nothing else could fill. She missed David. Even though she'd ended the relationship, she still checked her phone religiously to see if there were any texts or calls from him. But there were none.

"Hey, what are you doing?"

Jasmine looked up to see Alicia, drop into the chair opposite her. "Nothing."

"Don't tell me that. I saw you looking at your phone. You miss him, don't you? Then why did you break up with him?"

"I just thought—"

"Thought what? Jasmine, you know better than to make a major decision under the influence, which is exactly what you did with the anesthetic cocktail running through your veins. I love you dear, but you made a big mistake this time around. And how could you break up with him without giving him a chance to explain himself?

"I was hurt."

"True, and not thinking clearly."

Jasmine covered her face with her hands. "What am I going to do? I'm not sure he'll let me back into his life. Have you seen him recently?"

"I saw him in the ER today."

"How was he? I hope he was okay."

"Do you want to know?"

Jasmine nodded.

"Then fix this."

"How do I do that?"

"You figure it out, Ms. Take-the-Bull-by-the-Horns."

CHAPTER 43

*D*avid stood and stared out the window in his office. He'd arrived early because he'd had yet another sleepless night. The blue sky was tinged with hues of salmon pink and vibrant yellow as the sun awoke and rose high above the clouds. Which reminded him of Jasmine.

She had shone bright in his life, driving away the grayness that had been a constant companion since Heather died. He'd realized that he loved her and wanted to spend the rest of his life with her. But she'd cut him off instead. He hadn't been the same since then, and he missed her with an ache that wouldn't go away.

Everything else that involved her seemed to be going well.

The proposal they'd worked on had been approved by Prof. Morgan and submitted to the NIH. They expected to hear back soon about it.

Dr. Mallory—the surgeon that had taken over Jasmine's care since Dr. Lee had returned to LA—had assured him that Jasmine was healing nicely with no complications.

Jasmine's mom had also confirmed she was responding well to her medications and had started moving about. As much as he wanted to be with her, it was more important that nothing distressed or hampered her healing process in the immediate post-surgery period. So he'd stayed away.

But it was time to make things right between them. He couldn't wait any longer and needed to clear the misunderstanding that stood as a rock between them. He was certain she cared for him no matter what she'd said at the hospital. God had sent her back into his life, and he wasn't going to lose her easily.

He knew exactly what to do.

He picked up his phone from the desk and made a call.

Jasmine stopped to catch her breath as she entered her parents' house and shut the door behind her. She'd just taken a walk around the block with her mom, and she couldn't believe how exhausted she was. The surgery had definitely done a number on her.

Her mother had dropped her off, citing the need to pick up a gardening book from one of their neighbors. For some reason, it couldn't wait till the next day. Her mom was obsessed with gardening like that.

Her head jerked as a musical sound reached her ears. Were those notes from an acoustic guitar? And why did it seem like it was coming from the garden? No one was supposed to be at home. Her father had gone to the office and wasn't expected back by now. It could only be an intruder.

Jasmine swung the coat closet open and searched for the large umbrella that was always there. She wasn't sure how she would fare with her martial arts skills given her current state, but she would do her best.

She tiptoed as she made her way to the French doors that led to the garden. Her chest hurt, and she stopped to take steady breaths till it eased. Then she slowly cracked one of the doors open and slipped through it. The music got louder and seemed to be coming from the direction of the gazebo, which was usually empty except when her mom took editorial pictures of newly designed lingerie for the look book. Her feet crunched a little on the gravel that had rolled down from the flower hedge, but she ignored it.

And then her heart caught in her throat as she recognized the music. Could it be? She'd heard the song for the first time many years ago when she had dated David. It was a song he'd written just for her. But how?

And then she heard that voice, and the butterflies in her stomach woke up. It was David! But what was he doing here, and how had he gotten in? She'd thought she'd never see him again.

She quickened her steps till the gazebo came into full view, sparkling with tiny lights that gave it an ethereal look. David sat in the center on the stone bench, singing while playing the guitar.

She'd missed this view. He looked so good, wearing a light blue button-down shirt with rolled-up sleeves over dark jeans and custom Italian boots. Jasmine came to a halt, entranced both by the song and the sight of David. Her eyes locked into his, and he sang for her, the music weaving its way into the depths of her soul.

The song finally came to an end. He dropped the guitar on the bench, rose, and strode toward her.

Jasmine's heart pounded in her chest as each step brought him closer to her. He stopped when he was only a few steps away, his mesmerizing eyes focused on her.

Her mouth went dry. She didn't know what

to say, but she had to say something. "David, I—"

"Would it be okay if I spoke first?" David said softly.

Jasmine nodded and waited for him to continue.

"Jasmine, when I came back to Dexington, I didn't know what to expect. I was hurting from Heather's loss and had only planned to concentrate on my career and nothing else. But God had other plans." He gave her a soft smile.

Her insides melted. Was he going in the direction she was thinking? Her heart quickened its pace.

"You breezed into my life and turned it upside down," he continued. "The more time we spent together, the more I realized that you complete me. I'm sorry I wasn't there when you had the surgery. I had to fly to LA to handle another emergency surgery on Dr. Lee's behalf."

What did he mean by that? Could it be …? She gasped. He'd made it happen. She'd been surprised by how quickly Dr. Lee's schedule had opened up, but it hadn't occurred to her he'd been the one behind it. He'd done it, just for her.

Tears pooled behind her eyelids. "You should have told me," she said.

"I tried but I couldn't reach you. After I completed the surgery, I only went to Heather's grave to say goodbye. I needed closure with her. That way, I could make a fresh start with you. And I wanted to tell her I had found someone special like she'd urged me to, someone whose smile and laughter brighten my day, someone who makes my heart pound every day just the way I like it."

David took a few steps forward till he was standing right in front of her, his citrusy sandalwood scent embracing and warming her.

Jasmine's knees grew weak, and the umbrella slipped from her hands. She couldn't believe her ears, but she had to know more.

"David, what about Dr. Lee?"

"What about her?"

"Do you have a very close relationship with her?"

David laughed. "We are just good colleagues. Nothing inappropriate. Dr. Lee has two kids and a husband she adores. Were you jealous?"

Jasmine lifted her chin. "No, I wasn't."

David chuckled. "If you say so."

Then his face grew serious. "Jasmine, you are the only woman I want in my life, the only one I want to spend the rest of my life with. I want to wake up each day, hold you in my arms, and watch you become the best gynecologist you could ever be. And I love you as you are, cancer or not, even with the new twins." He winked at her.

Jasmine laughed. This man right here in front of her was special.

David pulled out a small black box from his pocket and opened it. It was like a million tiny diamonds twinkled from the exquisite ring that rested inside. Then he bent on one knee.

Jasmine gasped and held her hands over her mouth. This was really happening. She pinched herself, and it hurt. It wasn't a dream.

"Jasmine Banks, I love you very much, with all my heart. You are the woman for me, and I will be there for you in sickness and in health. We are in this together. Will you marry me?"

Jasmine's heart almost exploded at the words. This man standing in front of her loved her, despite the fact she was a cancer survivor. She stared into his eyes and saw the love brimming there. Her eyes stung as tears threatened to escape. "I'm sorry I drove you away. I was afraid you didn't care for me. I didn't know."

"Hey, don't cry. You are perfect just the way you are. I consider myself lucky to have met you. So will you marry me? I promise I won't drive you crazy."

Jasmine nodded amidst the tears that had run down her cheeks. "Yes, I'll marry you."

"Woohoo!" David grabbed her in a bear hug and twirled her around.

"Put me down. You are crushing me!" she said with laughter in her voice.

"Oh, sorry, I forgot," he said as he put her down gently like she was the most treasured thing in the world. He held her in his arms, beaming from ear to ear. And then he leaned closer till their noses touched.

Jasmine's breath caught, and the butterflies in her stomach fluttered. And then his lips touched hers in a soft and delicate way, like hers were a flower to be treasured. She pulled his head closer, her skin tingling where her hands touched his neck. The kiss was heady, intoxicating, and she craved more. And then he deepened the kiss, and the butterflies in her belly went crazy. It was like she was flying, soaring, high above everything else.

"Son, let the girl breathe."

Jasmine's head jerked in the direction of the sound. "Did I just hear your father's voice?"

That was when she saw her parents, David's parents, Alicia, Blake, Willow, Dana, and Josh walking toward them. "Surprise!" they screamed.

Jasmine was at a loss for words for a moment. "When did you guys—"

"Get here?" her mom completed her question. "We've been here the whole time."

Jasmine's face grew red, and she hid her face in the crook of David's neck. This was so embarrassing. David chuckled and rubbed her back, which, by the way, felt really good.

"Mommy, I like Uncle Dave," Willow quipped, her voice loud enough above the excited chatter from everyone.

Jasmine turned to look at her. Willow was dressed in a long-sleeved fuchsia wool dress that highlighted the blue color of her eyes, an impish smile on her face.

"Why?" Alicia asked as she looked down at Willow.

"Because he knows how to kiss, just like you and Daddy Blake."

"Willow!" Alicia said as everyone burst into laughter.

Jasmine smiled and winked at Willow. She had the best man in the world and her family around her.

The day could not be more perfect.

CHAPTER 45

Jasmine snuck a peek at the large room from where she stood in the wings. The ballroom had been transformed into a runway fit for a fashion show.

The Landisil-IntimiRose acquisition had gone through, and a fashion show had been selected as the stage to kick off the first joint collection. There had been much buzz in the news about it, and a lot of work had gone into its planning. Jasmine had even lent a hand despite her busy schedule.

She could see all the hard work had paid off. The rows of seats lining each side of the platform were completely filled with no standing room. Lots of cameras clicked away as the models walked down the runway, showing off the new bra designs from the new Landisil-IntimiRose collection.

The designs were exquisite, with the signature Intimi-Rose floral nuance, and orders for them were already flooding in. All the models for the show were breast cancer survivors, with the profits from the collection donated to support breast cancer research. Jasmine hoped the successful completion of the event would bring more breast cancer awareness.

Her friends had come to lend their support. Alicia, Blake, Dana, and Josh sat in the second row and watched the show with keen interest. Willow had begged to attend, but Alicia had refused, saying she wasn't ready for the next harebrained idea Willow might come up with from it. Dana had already slipped Jasmine a note with the designs she wanted to lock down for her honeymoon trip.

She spotted David in one of the front row seats, his parents and her parents flanking him on either side. He winked at her before turning his attention back on the stage. Jasmine could feel her face heating up. This was the kind of effect David had on her. She loved this man with all her heart and couldn't imagine anyone else in her life.

And today had been a double blessing. They had just received news that they'd won the research grant. It was like the icing on the cake of such a wonderful day.

And then the show's director told her the finale had arrived. It was time for her to walk.

Jasmine took a deep breath, lifted her chin, and took to the runway.

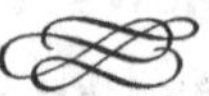

Jasmine watched as David cradled their newborn and sang softly to her while they waited for the pediatrician. Olivia Grace smiled and kicked her feet in return. A warmth radiated through Jasmine's chest at the sight.

She still couldn't believe she'd had a baby a few weeks ago. She'd had two rounds of chemotherapy a few months after her double mastectomy and had been fortunate to only lose her hair as a side effect. She'd grown it back into a pixie cut which she now loved. No additional cancer cells had been found so far in her bi-yearly checkups. And her marriage hadn't suffered from the loss of her breasts as she'd feared.

She'd opted not to have kids because of the high risk of passing the BRCA gene mutation, so she hadn't frozen her eggs before the chemotherapy.

But God had other plans. She'd gotten pregnant as she was finishing up her Gynecologic Oncology fellowship, despite the birth control she'd been placed on after her wedding. They'd been worried the whole time and were here to find out Olivia Grace's genetic test results.

The door opened behind them. The pediatrician walked in and sat down at his desk. He checked something on his computer screen and then looked at them with a solemn expression.

Jasmine's heart nosedived, and her stomach churned. *God, please, let it not be true.*

The doctor cleared his throat. "Drs. Landi, the results show that your baby does not have the BRCA gene mutation."

Jasmine let out the breath she didn't know she'd held. *Thank you, God.* The mutation had ended with her.

David bent to kiss their baby's face, and Jasmine noticed his cheeks were wet. She dug into her bag and handed him a handkerchief. "We just need a minute," she told the doctor.

When David calmed down, he turned to Jasmine. "I'm going to get a vasectomy. I can't go through this again. It almost killed me."

She smiled back at him. "Okay." She understood how he felt, and she rubbed his shoulder. Olivia Grace had been a miracle and was more than enough for them.

"Congratulations!" the doctor said.

Jasmine smiled. "Thank you."

Her life couldn't be more full. She had a future, a precious baby to dote on, and the man she loved by her side.

Her very own Billionaire Army Doc.

Thank you so much for reading! Want to know what happens next in Dexington, and how Gabriella, David's sister, found love (in a best-friend's sister romance)?

Check out LOVING THE BILLIONAIRE BOSS DOC at https://dobidaniels.com.

Here's an excerpt:

"Watch out!"

Gabriella looked up to see herself careening toward an old lady crossing the road right ahead of her, who seemed oblivious to her surroundings. Gabriella pressed the brakes to slow down, but it wasn't enough. The old woman was coming up too close!

Suddenly, strong arms grabbed her handle bars and steered them toward the sidewalk. The bike swayed and then collapsed, and Gabriella found herself landing on a solid mass of muscle. The darkest pair of brown eyes she'd ever seen stared back at her. There was something familiar about them, like she'd known them a long time ago, though she couldn't remember where or how.

"Ma'am, are you alright?" asked a beautiful baritone voice that made her heart skip a beat.

Her face grew warm, and she scrambled off him. "I'm so sorry … thank you … I didn't mean …" She looked to see the old lady had made it safely to the other side of the road. Thank goodness. Then she turned back to her savior.

The man, who looked to be in his early thirties, got up and dusted the beige spring trench coat he wore over his suit. He could very well have been a model for a high-end men's magazine with the effortless way his clothes framed his body. Gabriella was still a sucker for good-looking, well-dressed men, though she'd learned her lesson not to judge a book solely by its cover.

"Are you alright?" he asked, the hint of a British accent coming through. It was just her luck. Why did she have to encounter her deadliest combination today? Who wouldn't swoon at a gorgeous man with a British accent?…

Want to read more? You can grab LOVING THE BILLIONAIRE BOSS DOC at https://dobidaniels.com!

Or want to know what happens next in Dexington?
Sign up now at https://dobidaniels.com.

If you've loved reading Loving the Billionaire Army Doc, Dobi would be grateful if you could spend a few minutes to leave a review (as short as you like) on the book's page on your favorite retailer. Your review would help bring it to the attention of other readers. Thank you very much.

Check out all Dobi Daniels books at https://dobidaniels.com

ACKNOWLEDGMENTS

Writing a book is harder and more rewarding than I could have ever imagined. And it would not have been possible without the support, love, and encouragement from my number one cheerleader, my dearest mom. My life would never have been this awesome and wonderful without you.

Of course, I have to thank my precious little DC for his smiles and antics. You brighten my day and give me the strength to keep pushing through.

Thank you to my sisters for encouraging me on this wonderful journey. And a special thanks to my baby brother (who is so not a baby anymore) for being super supportive and checking in on my progress. You guys are the best.

Thank you to my wonderful author friends. You know who you are. Your selflessness and willingness to share what you know has made my writing journey smoother and an exciting one. And a special thanks to Lisa and Deanna whose support have made a difference.

Most of all, I want to thank God who gave me life, surrounded me with the most wonderful people, and loved me all the way. You make my life complete.

And finally, a special thanks to all my readers whose love of my stories spur me on to write more. Thank you!

As a former physician and business executive in another life—with a childhood filled with reading multi-genre novels—Dobi Daniels loves to write sweet thrilling romance stories with heart. She enjoys dreaming up everyday characters who rise above unfavorable circumstances to overcome incredible odds and find joy along the way.

When not writing, Dobi can be found binging K-dramas and ice cream with her little sidekick by her side.

Loving the Billionaire Army Doc is the third book in the Dexington Doctor Billionaires Series. Sign up at dobidaniels.com to be notified when the next Dobi Daniels book comes out!

Thank you!